THE
VELOCITY
GOSPEL

ACCOMPLICE 2

STEVE AYLETT

GOLLANCZ
LONDON

The right of Steve Aylett to be identified as the author
of this work has been asserted by him in accordance
with the Copyright, Designs and Patents Act 1988.

This edition first published in Great Britain in 2002 by
Gollancz
An imprint of the Orion Publishing Group
Orion House, 5 Upper St Martin's Lane,
London WC2H 9EA

A CIP catalogue record for this book
is available from the British Library

ISBN 0 575 07088 9

Typeset at The Spartan Press Ltd,
Lymington, Hants

Printed in Great Britain by
Clays Ltd, St Ives plc

25/5

THE
VELOCITY
GOSPEL

WOK	
WOO	
LOW	
MAI	6.02
SPE	
TWY	
CON	4/03
WAR	9/02
MOB	
EHS	
RES	

Steve Aylett is author of *The Crime Studio,*
Bigot Hall, Slaughtermatic, The Inflatable Volunteer,
Toxicology, Shamanspace, Atom and
Only an Alligator.

Visit the author's website at:
www.steveaylett.com

For And

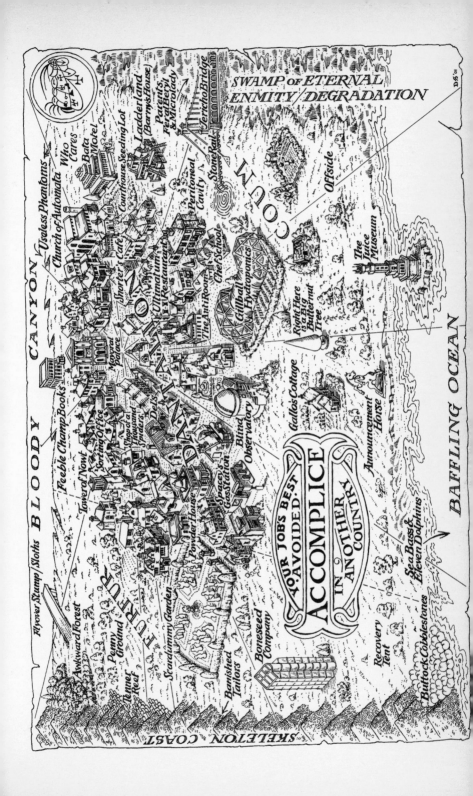

John's head exploded during cremation and everyone heard it but pretended otherwise. There'll always be an England.

Punching the Sarge

When someone tells you life's a dream, you can bet they're about to inconvenience you very badly. I was watching when Barny Juno stole a small midday snack from the forces of evil, thus setting in motion a series of adventures which still amuse and appal people with time on their hands. It pulled monsters into the world like meat from a shellfish, all white to the sun. Why didn't I interfere? Just before my death I did nip in with a prophecy regarding the demon who was eating my head at the time. But backbone needs a body. Since I abandoned the daily business of human anatomy I've spied from an etheric sideband, cosy and floating. Accomplice was a tropic of slack-jawed nutters. Justice as rare as a jelly fossil. And Barny couldn't concentrate on the evil at hand. Mind elsewhere and nothing furtive. A manchild whose life had slipped into a casual fairy tale. As the heated air fluttered like a ghost.

1

Never Talk to Strangers

A story is ready when it falls out of your face

A massive hot ruby hung steaming in space a country mile beneath Accomplice. Its heart a turning red rind, it added colour to the skull-studded extravaganza of air pain and spinelight in that neck of the world. Lounging in a veined halfshell, a white mantid ghoul with complicated mouthparts had a famous time distributing nightmares and inconvenience through a network of thick coaxial nerve cables. Sweeney's egg eyes and huge blown head like the skull of a whale – this was the first face a fool would see after getting his arse caught in the drum of a player piano.

Branched glimpses of electricity banged across the walls and floor of the titanic cavern. 'Night is never terminal,' Sweeney sighed, turning his attention to the boulder-sized gemstone. 'Where is the man Barny Juno?'

'He is among a crowd of people.'

'What's he doing.'

'He searches for a snake . . .'

The old blood clock counterweighted into motion and two mechanical knights propelled on to a narrow platform. As the blue and yellow figures clashed swords, Mayor Rudloe stepped on to the balcony above and regarded the broth of humanity which had gathered in the sun-white town square. Most of them were staring up at the palace like gooney-birds. The Mayor ballooned out, speaking. 'I have asked you to infest this square in order to impart warning of a dire threat to our community. I've been passing myself off as the big authority round here for years. You granted me that honour at breakneck speed, all almond-eyed and eager. You turn in unison like pinstripe fish and I bless you for it. Maintaining m'stranglehold here's the only exercise my brachioradial muscles ever get. Boy, is it ever sweet. But as Accomplice's single organ of government and frankly the only man with any ideas around here, I must talk to you regarding certain bastards who would defame our imploded society. They call themselves the Followers of Cyril. A ravening rabble lacking the gratitude which most of us take for granted, they are workshy and pensive – and probably, if they've got any sense, armed to the teeth. Strictly speaking this is baseless but I love it. Revolution – how the cured thing dooms the rest of us. They're playing merry hell with everything and this half-arsed development couldn't have come at a better time. There's a red deficit – isn't it a pity? The mechanised knights below, ever toiling in their faithful service, require an extra bloody tribute to keep them clashing. I wept lard this morning as I thought of how vexing and costly it will be for you. Then I carved the lard into the shape of a raven. So you see how I put you people first? Nothing is wasted. I save on expense by shrugging with only one shoulder. Get a loada this – heyup.'

Down among the socket-faced masses Barny Juno and the gangling Plantin Edge were discussing corpse praline and radio cartoons in an absent sort of way. Barny looked moon-faced and wondering through the crowd and occasionally crouched amid their shuffling legs. Plantin Edge was wearing a sheet and eating popcorn in the Accomplice heat. 'So you went to the Garden with Madge yesterday, Bubba?'

Barny looked uncomfortable. 'I had to borrow a book from someone. I've been boning up on moths. I reckon the one I ate was a geometrid. Maybe Fang could find a replacement for me – he's a bug man.'

'He's a *bog* man. And you borrowed a book, eh? I get it. From that little fringed musette at the Juice Museum.'

Barny sighed dismally. 'We pranced all happy through some of the big flowers they've got round there. She's . . . limber. Bendy. Fang says I've only got one tongue and I might as well use it.'

'So what's the problem?'

'Magenta Blaze. She's convinced I'm an interesting man and won't let go of my leg.'

'You're sure you want Chloe Low at the Juice?'

'I agree with all of her heart, Edgy. I can't explain it.'

Edgy crammed popcorn and thought. 'Get around to Beltane Carom. He'll give you some arcane and surefire method of dumping the Blaze.'

'At least he's not one of those gurus who thinks he's funny. They're the pits.'

'Yeah, and everyone's too respectful to tell them? No, he's a shaman, Bubba, a master. He's giving me some advice about Amy. You know she wants me to help her publish that terrible poetry of hers, like I've got any influence on old Crash Test Nureyev over the publishers? The wand jockey listened to the problem and set me straight. His nose was pullulating the whole time.'

'So what did he say?'

Edgy frowned in recollection. 'The object of many dimensions is to make all things ignorable by a simple manoeuvre.'

'What does that mean? Is this stupid sheet part of it?'

'No, I was halfway through a haunting at the motel when I heard about this little shindig. Well I had to come along, Bubba. You remember last time? That massive galvanised tin head eating the populace? The bite radius on the thing, boy oh boy. For all his faults the Mayor knows how to put on a show.'

'Why's he going on about his shoulder?' Barny muttered, preoccupied with peering amid the crowd.

'Could it be otherwise? Misdirection, Bubba. Look at him. Too sure to look shifty. Unencumbered by memory of his mistakes, the man's cheeks are completely out of control.'

Barny glanced up. 'His bones are coming through his mouth.'

'Those are his teeth. They live to serve him.'

'I don't understand what he's talking about.'

'You're not supposed to. What did old Bingo Violaine say? Deflate a gasbag at your peril.'

'Right now I'm just worried about Misses Kennedy. This is no place for a puff adder, Edgy. Really big vipers need shelter and care. She's excited now but she'll get anxious later. I caught her tanning in the sandwich maker and she must have thought I was angry and ran away. Put a centre parting in the lawn by the roundabout. Maybe she's nervous about the contest. She's around here somewhere, maybe under some cycads.'

'She'll be fine. Hey, Barny, can I go hang with the leopard with you? I think I could handle it, you know, if he took a swipe at me with his paw.'

'Well, Edgy, treat him with respect. His ears might be velvet but he has mood swings that'll make your chin stand on end.'

'You're the best friend the winged and stepping animals of the earth could have, Bubba, but you should chill out.

Take some popcorn. It always reminds me of little skulls or something.'

'You know if they were real and had some meat on them, they might tempt Misses Kennedy. Are you sure it's just popcorn?'

Edgy sifted through the carton. 'It's a needle in a haystack.' He emptied the carton on to the ground. 'There – if there's a skull we know who'll find it, eh? Lateral thinking.'

'I never would have thought of that.' Barny nodded in frank admiration. Edgy had a sharp mind in that tall, tufted head of his.

Barny squatted amid the forest of legs and squeaked a beckoning call to the serpent.

'Hey, you know who I can see, Bubba?' Edgy called down to him, and squinted over the assembly. A keg-shaped man with a head like a potato stared up at the mayoral palace in rapt attention. 'It's Gregor. Yeah, he's right at the front of the crowd. It looks like he's really into it. Hey, Round One!'

The cry registered dimly on the Mayor's consciousness and, thinking it referred to him, he discarded it. 'We have yet to see the Followers of Cyril in the full bloom of atrocity,' he was saying. 'I don't pretend to understand their contempt. I'll not deceive you, I regard new systems of humour with suspicion.

'Accomplice is a community unto itself. Be vigilant. At a time of social emergency it's crucial to abstain from riots as irksome to me as their necessity is to you. It is written here in our Constitution' – and the Mayor dabbled his fingers in a tray of water – 'that money's an opinion we daren't lose. However, the good news is, I can help you. First I declare a state of constant readiness. I will decide in due course that the levy must be increased to counter the baleful crisis. At that time I will set upon a policy greatly at odds with your wellbeing, squashing your faces as though against a rippled pane of glass. This will be followed by a root and branch review, a clamour of ear-grinding excuses and, finally, the really back-breaking work of denying everything. One or two timid witnesses will drift down a river and deal out into the sea. Then I'll give a big horselaugh. We haven't a moment to lose. I foresee a land positively blistering with safety. One of green television fields and beaches shut with tides. Pearls barricade the advancement steps, cranks watch summer from the porch. Working hands down, you shroud the dying in laughter. Exhaustions brow the night. Rejoice. These lofty notions are food and drink to you aimless wonders. You're supported, you're safe, you're happy—'

'You're okay!' yelled Barny, raising the venomous adder above the crowd. The assembly exploded outward like the primal bang. Screams wheeled and intersected as hundreds legged it and Edgy's sheet was torn away in the commotion.

Before the Mayor was fully aware of events, he was gazing down at an almost deserted town square. Only three people remained – the man with the deadly viper, a naked man who stood like a used match, and a spudlike creature who stared silently up with a look of gluey need. This last one, the Mayor realised with alarm, was playing pocket billiards. The other two seemed to understand this at the same moment and, rushing forward, bundled the round man away.

The clock knights, swords locked in silence, finally disengaged and swerved backwards, doors of red gold flipping closed upon them.

'Business as usual above,' Sweeney ruminated, turning from the Ruby. 'But see how Juno and the scarecrow ran to the aid of their piglike friend, the creature they call the Round One. A weak link?'

'Juno's kept aloft and unreachable,' said Dietrich the Hammer, entering the cavern astride a scuttling legal cadaver, 'on the thermals of his own ignorance.' He drew to a stop, all membrane wings and stained armour.

Sweeney clacked his shoehorn tongue. 'I've a mind to send Skittermite above.'

Dietrich twitched his tomahawk head to peer at the emperor grub. 'Kermit?' he spat.

'He's been punching below his weight for a while now. Not still stuck in that pipe I suppose?'

'Exactly. If he hadn't the wherewithal to avoid the simplest drain, how could he navigate Accomplice? It's chaotic beyond endurance up there – because those bastards are completely covered in skin, they think they can deny their insides.'

The sheer architectural extravagance of demonic biology was mostly open to inspection, infernodyne veins and pulsing bile yolk fully visible through wide-flung ribs.

'You want to go back, after Juno's sucker-punch?' Sweeney leered like a burning snowman. 'One of the best tunes and you've changed it. You didn't used to think he was worth the candle. Pegged him as a simpleton.'

'So he is – a man "simple and true", like the prophecy of your downfall, Your Majesty.'

'Please don't complicate such a simple matter. Fetch the imp.'

Skittermite was tossing shoes into the smelter when Dietrich came for him. Victim blood still draining from his gills, he scurried after the bigger fiend like a charbroiled monkey, all pickbones and shoulderblades. From his wedge-shaped head projected two thin prongs, useful only for toasting mallows.

Sweeney turned as they entered. Magnesium glares lit the heat-blasted cowling of his skull. 'Pay close attention, flydart.'

Skittermite deployed his ears, flapping them like sparrow wings. Dietrich stood by with a twitching face.

'You and your telescopic canines are going above to Accomplice. Barny Juno needs aggravating unto death. He's hex-protected so nix on the gnash, we need to operate through the social grind. Luckily there's a political push on the go and mugs will be out in force. Concentrate on the man with the body of a potato, this barrel being they call the Round One. He's got a medical bracelet that says "Just throw me away". I believe he's the vulnerable point in Juno's entourage. So get some scars, prove you're not too new for the job. Need any of these?' Sweeney indicated a wall of human faces which he called his 'personality pelts'.

'Please no your Majesty thank you,' Skittermite sibilated.

'Good, well, left and right, space is limitless – manipulation therefore is limitless. Dietrich here seems to think they dislike being tackled by the legs – you might try that.'

'Thank you. By your command.' Skittermite dipped his wedge-shaped head.

'Off you go then.'

Skittermite darted up a slope as though launched from a spring-winder, chittering his joy.

Dietrich sullenly picked the eye from his mount – it squirmed in his hand like a fizzing Tylenol. As a paravamp demon his own eyes registered all one and a half thousand shades of black but he could not understand the worth of Accomplice.

'You've been grinding your head about the place,' stated Sweeney, 'since Gettysburg went renegade. You misplace blame. Getty was a good seed, that's all.'

Dietrich looked at the ivory king insect in wonder. It was rare for Sweeney to mention the defector's name. The demon Gettysburg had started his conscientious objecting covertly by inventing the rule that to be invoked, his name must be repeated 86,400 times. Most people got bored or fell asleep before hitting the number and this gave him years to kick back and hang in the fiery deeps. The invocation procedure was clearly useless in an emergency and Sweeney queried it, but Gettysburg insisted that it was sly and evil since it led to people using his name casually and without regard. He claimed that the unsuspecting would one day cumulatively hit the magic number and find themselves confronted by the mirror-eyed shrike. His excuses for mellow behaviour became lamer by the decade. Finally he went out for cigarettes and never returned.

'I've walked the floors of oceans,' Dietrich explained, 'and passed finer society.'

'Look closer. I've known their world, leather to feathers. I even witnessed the grim, fateful appearance of the first herb. Mankind mines a stratum of the obvious so thick it occupies their lifetime. And more good news – every inch of flesh is carvable.'

The Mayor walked in off the balcony and picked among the floor lobsters toward his darkwood desk. These large armoured roaches, physical evidence of spiritual corruption, had monopolised the floor space since the cleaner died. Rudloe kicked one gingerly and it curled up like an ammonite. It also resembled, the Mayor reflected vaguely, a cat which was quite at home. 'I expected more merriment,' he said, sitting down.

'Well, sir, pocket billiards,' remarked the lawyer Max Gaffer. 'What could be more merry?'

'I looked away for a split second and the populace was

reduced to a child-faced moron with a venomous snake, a rather gormless, uninspired flasher and a round man utterly absorbed with his own balls. Everyone else had done a runner.'

'In record time.'

'That's no consolation, I'm afraid. Who was the one with the death-adder? Have I met him?'

'Barny Juno. He's the guy who held a funeral for a lizard and dropped his trousers during the eulogy. Came in here dressed as an ape. Flies around on a swan.'

'This is all one man?'

'He's a notorious mooncalf, Mayor. A spooky simpleton. Doesn't know enough to stop. Irritates everyone, up to and including our lord the devil himself.'

'You seen him on the swan?'

'Swans are very graceful.'

'So that's a no. Wait a second, this the guy I demonised a while back? Well there's your proof, Max. Inventing a nebulous enemy's the rage. We'll never have Cyril barging in here in a monkey suit, the bastard doesn't exist.'

'Outstanding, sir.' The lawyer, whose yellow eyes and fishbone hairstyle unnerved the living, conceded that the Cyril mirage was a sound tactic. The Mayor had been in a weakened position since going out on a limb with his 'I am a Beautiful Woman' campaign. Almost everyone agreed he had overstepped the mark, and those who had expressed hearty support became abashed and furtive. The new trap was spare and inexpensive. 'Just keep 'em blaming.'

'Well, I've planted the seed. Get old Turbot to write us another speech, turning up the heat. Behind thick manoeuvres I'll reduce my efforts. The scrap cost can be disregarded. The promises? Forgot into our pockets again. As Violaine said, timing is the knowledge that society may have been more ready in the past than in the present. Even the waking collective attributes tyranny to the assigned villain.'

The Mayor struck a match on the armour of a passing bug and lit a cigar. The big wheel always came around.

2

Foghorn Mother

A camel cannot be impressed

Barny worked part-time at the Sorting Office, a pressure chamber of swarming embers and anxiety. His co-workers, Edgy and Gregor included, amused themselves with muted but erudite comparisons of snot coloration. Never-admitted ignorance as to the nature of the job filled everyone with stressful dread and morbid evasion. In fact the stress was of such consistent quality that a clown cartel once attempted to harvest it via quick-blooming nerve pumps fed through the damp walls. When finally a test subject sampled the harvest, his face exploded and showered the onlookers with flaming tar.

Today Barny entered the basement to find that though the morning had thus far passed without bloodshed, their hale supervisor, the Captain, had swung by to find Gregor living it up to the exclusion of all else. The Captain's expression was as clenched and grim as he could muster in the damp heat of the day. 'Jeepers creepers, boys, couldn't you keep a friendly eye on this guy? Gregor baby, we all thought you'd made a clean start of it until you decided to astound everyone with your behaviour in the square. From what I heard, you yelled something, tore off your clothes and started waving a demonically over-sized whanger about the place. By golly, man – staring directly into the Mayor's eyes the whole time? Aren't you remotely satisfied by your work here?'

'Not the Mayor.'

'Eh?'

'I wasn't looking at the Mayor and . . . let's just leave it at that.'

Something drew the Captain's eyes to a corner of the gloomy basement. Gregor had used a load of the baffling papers and packages which poured daily into the office to create a full-sized papier-mâché effigy of one of the town clock knights. 'Holy mackerel. On probation from your past and here I find you've been out lusting after concrete figurines after all. By jimminy, can't a week pass without me having to fire one of you fellas? Come on.'

'You're firing me?' Gregor mumbled. 'Shouldn't I be praised for trying to get it out of my system?'

'Gregor, your motives are as obscure as a spider's face, and much as I love you and wish you well, nothing'll ever escape a system as warped and twisted as I see you displaying here. You know I answer to Mr Gibbon. I wonder why I waited this long. And more importantly—'

And the Captain skipped up the stairs, slamming out.

'I wish he wouldn't do that,' said Edgy.

'Well, for some fantastic reason he's gone weird in the head and fired me.' Gregor laughed uneasily, looking worried at the others. 'Eh? It's probably illegal, right?'

'No, he's got you bang to rights,' said BB Henrietta.

Edgy was jittery and startled, looking at Gregor with newly troubled eyes. 'Hey it never occurred to any of us you were looking at those mechanical knights, Round

One. I thought you built this thing in the corner just to get rid of some paper stuff. You'll get a cornerstone order for this. It's way worse than when you forced yourself on those dinosaur remains.'

'How can you like something that was never alive?' asked Barny with genuine curiosity. 'It's like them creepy Church of Automata people.'

Gregor made a disconsolate sound. There was general, appalled agreement that he had gone too far. Though known to one and all as a man who inhabited a species for which he was manifestly unqualified, he had caught everyone off-guard with this lust for a juddering trophy. 'I only like the blue one,' he protested, and immediately knew he'd said the worst.

'Can you hear yourself?'

Backs were turning, including that of Fang, a zombie whose spine-knurls were horribly visible and quite compelling.

'This mean I've got to move out of the maintenance cupboard?' Gregor asked wanly.

Nobody replied. Gregor released a small whimper.

Skittermite buzzed out of the creepchannel on a gristle bike, slewing to a stop in a spray of blown watches. Hunkering down to eat the engine, he pondered the hot, ripe land about him. A scarlet countryside, earth crammed with tea, funerals . . . He was finally going to the show. Some saw Accomplice as a skull, a domain bound by bone and notion. To Skitter it seemed a fertile arena. Angel refineries stood like gravestones and rotten hearts were piled in the sabotage yard. Electric with mischief and anticipation, he resolved to acquit himself well. His plan was to understand the way of things here, blend in and imitate. Then the horror.

*

That night Gregor slept in a tough leather sack slung from a tree branch. Once again he'd eaten his luck like a tie spooned up with the morning cereal.

Gravel flew against the bag – he unzipped and looked into the night. The pale face of Barny Juno looked up at him, whispering urgently. 'Gregor – sorry about this morning. I don't know why I went along with it. Take some advice and don't tell anyone I told you.'

'What is it?'

'Maybe that Church of Automata will know what to do about them mechanical dummies, if you convince them your problems are creepy enough. And you can stay at my place. This tree's for losers.'

'Ladderland? I'm not staying in that overgrown barn of yours – the lion'll drag me apart and the howler monkeys'll piss on my cadaver.'

'I'm reading about silverbacked apes,' hissed Barny. 'Those mothers monitor the location and activity of the gorillas in their group, decide when and where the group will move, and settle arguments among the females.'

'Have you got anything relevant to add? No? Then don't bother me any more.'

A few minutes later more gravel splashed against the bag – Gregor looked down to see the wiry form of Edgy. 'Gregor – sorry about this morning. I don't know why I went along with it. Take some advice and don't tell anyone I told you.'

'What advice?'

'Go to Stampede Door to Door and tell them I sent you – they'll give you a job. As for all the other stuff, try to rise above it by spurting pints of saliva at your more sedate adversaries. Puzzle all with a new chin. It's a stellar choice. That way they'll remember you.'

'That's exactly what I don't want.'

'Why?' whispered Edgy.

'Well they'll either barge me with honours or single me out for derision, won't they? Either way my nerves'll be shot. Anyway I'm already looking for a job. Talked to Kenny Reactor at the gillball nursery – told me he could hear the vegetables crying out against me. He said if I didn't leave straight away, they'd start launching all premature.'

'A gut farmer? That's not the course of exhaustion for you, Round One. Go to the Stampede like I said. Goodnight.'

Edgy left and Gregor settled down. Soon another spray of gravel hit the bag and Gregor peered down blearily to see a thing which was basically a couple of walking elbows and a gob like a staple gun. This bony predator gaped a wound full of needles and chittered. 'Gregor – sorry about this morning. I don't know why I went along with it. Take some advice and don't tell anyone I told you—'

Gregor exploded from the tree, terror blasting from his mouth as he hit the ground running. The wedge-headed stranger seemed to implore behind him as he belted into the night. Gregor took it upon himself to scream as he tripped on an abandoned stove. When the hell would his expression be that of a normal man?

The following morning Barny visited the shaman Beltane Carom as Edgy had advised in the Square. Barny liked the shaman's mild manners and calm way of life. He had once seen Carom push an iron key into the surface of a flowing stream and pull up a transparent lid, reaching in to retrieve a choc ice.

Barny met him in a walled courtyard in which the flagstones were configured to a weightless pattern. The yard had its own sky and a corner pond of green shadow. Carom placed his nerve lute aside and asked what Barny had in mind.

'I need to break it off with Magenta Blaze. She's crazy

and I want to be with someone else I met. I can't overlap. What do I do?'

'If you continue with a broken chair, do you snub the truth or accept it?'

Barny shook his head slowly and sadly. 'I just don't know what you're talking about, ma'am.'

'Unfortunate – but true, at least. It's only some facts that a name will stick to – others are too slippery, fast or fierce. Let's see what the cards say.' Beltane produced a deck of blackstrap cards, irregular slabs of threaded meat and woven gristle. Each stacking order created one of twenty-seven different organs. 'To have and to hold, to cut out and keep. Let's see.' He began placing cards and reading their meanings. 'Seven cards. Fornix. "Slaves enter the box, all cities are at an end." Sarcomere. "Smoking a squirrel, I backed into the shed." The first-person statements address the matter of socially trans-gressive mirth, gold in the water. Buccinator. "He turns the sign against their questions."'

The cards lay like dry steaks, muted whorls and nephritic blemishes unreadable to Barny's eyes.

'Jejunum. "Through a dossier his decency runs like the thwarting shadow of a synagogue." Hypodermis. "By all means moan tonight." Trapezius. "My whisper outraged the debutante." Concha. "No one else is laughing." There you have it.'

'So what does it all mean?'

'Well, sometimes the truth's right there for you, Barny. Like the obvious fact that knees and potatoes are the same thing.'

'What for?'

'Emergencies maybe, that's not the point. This woman, Magenta Blaze, she's not listening – you can push through that self-involvement with something called the Power Shout.'

'Power Shout. How's it done?'

'When the time comes, you'll know. At the very least you'll frighten the life out of her.'

'That's all there is to it?'

'Well, freedom's funny. It looks green but it tastes red.' He began tossing the cards into the pond, where they were snapped down by sudden fish. 'What fury teaches is a candid superstructure to hold happiness. Was there something else you wanted to talk about, Barny? Something deeper?'

'I've put up Misses Kennedy for this year's Deadly Snake Competition. But I don't want her to be nervous or become ill. Everyone reckons she's in line for the Hold It In the Middle and Flinch But Don't Let Go When It Flexes Unpredictably rosette. Anyway, so Golden Sid, who takes care of the animals when I'm at work? He's the judge. But Balaclava Lewis, with his black mamba Tamale, he says there's partiality there, so for the moment Sid isn't allowed to work with me until after the contest. People sure are suspicious.'

'Right. So, er . . . is there anything else, Bubba, something troubling you, maybe about the family or some such?'

'There's the moth thing, yeah, my parents kept a moth in a canary cage, called it Ramone. I ate it by accident. They think I deliberately let it go to fly away. Why would I do that? Now I want to replace it without them knowing but I can't find the sort of geometrid moth I need.'

'The trickster, what's his name, he has a moth of that variety, which he keeps in his navel.'

'Yeah, you're sure?'

'He cavorts in the Square sometimes – seek him there. If he's not there he'll be behind the snout distillery. And don't take no for an answer.'

Barny was chuffed. 'Thank you, ma'am. You've been a real help.'

Barny couldn't find Prancer Diego in the Square so he went through the snout distillery toward his room. The distillery was a front for a flower store, which fronted a bar full of angry failures, which was in turn the front for a sauna. Behind this were the sequential fronts of a print shop, a karate school, a giant mouth, a movie theatre and a bowling alley. This all fronted a spartan room which had no back wall and was totally exposed to the air – anyone walking the street could see Prancer undressing for bed or sitting bolt upright in a wooden chair, semolina dripping from his ears.

When Barny arrived, Prancer was trying to step with both legs at once and straining with hilarity at his experiment. In this sort of useless activity Prancer was unmatched. He'd dig a shallow hole, do a headstand in it and claim he was wearing the entire world as a hat. He annoyed everyone by wearing nicotine patches on his eyes, talking almost perfectly through his nostrils and doing the Heimlich manoeuvre on people who were perfectly fine. In queuing to end his life at least a thousand people were turned away. When someone gave him the white feather of cowardice he used it to smudge his aura. His skull already made him a human, why did he have to learn the behaviour?

'Oho, Bubba,' Prancer hailed him. 'Sorry I'm late. A towering flume of winged demons spurted from a man-hole, delaying me.'

'What?'

'A word to the wise, Juniper. When you dislike a comment, chew the nose from the speaker. That way any of your more well-meaning friends may withdraw. And I heard about Gregor's stunt with his whanger. I'd like to shake his hand.'

'Rather you than me, Dago.'

'Reveal a gasp-causing body slain in sobs by a repressed monk. Works every time.'

'I suppose it's asking too much to expect a normal sentence from that gob of yours?'

Prancer dodged and ducked as though under attack, all in silence and peaceful circumstance.

'Er, anyway, I need the moth in your belly button, Dago. And no stupid games, it's important.'

Prancer's avian head nodded sagely. 'One day breath will be enough. But only by stealth. Cyril doesn't even exist. So to save our lovely Mayor the indignity of being branded a liar, we must create this being from air. You and your buddies could really help me out at a sedate pace.'

And Prancer suddenly wigged out real bad, grabbing Barny by the shirt and rushing him through the bowling alley, the movie theatre, the giant mouth and the karate school until, exploding into the printshop, he produced a bullhorn from nowhere and bellowed through it while priming the machinery. His manner was wild and truculent. 'Society. Bleed but don't make a scene. Mouths tuned to one story and useless leg advice. Some button head destiny selected from a list, maybe a little friend to point at the chicken dream as immobile creatures report their glued thoughts. Depend on bills, swallow corpses, greet business, die. This forehead of yours responds with fashion merely, fool's gold and fossilfruit.' Prancer tore off his own shirt, stancing heroically. 'Authority – let us do it the supreme honour of incessant disregard. The idea that we should somehow develop a good attitude is to be humoured, fantastical though it is. A stern code of tolerance may yet result from this exercise alone. Chain-smoke menus. Grow out of your size and get respect. Tomorrow I'll celebrate – today here's your neck to grab. I defy the idlers to sleep me out.'

Prancer wheeled aside, flinging himself on to the print machine. He hoisted down the spearlike axis of the bare drumholder so that it side-pierced his chest, burrowing through the flesh and nosing out of the other side.

Barny wished he was back amid the natural ferocity of his animals. 'Please, Dago, you're scaring me,' he shouted above the escalating rev of the machine.

'A society with the face of a priest!' Prancer laughed as the drum shaft began to turn, breaking the skin of his chest and rolling his flesh downward like a scroll.

'Dago, you must be sick.' Barny quailed as the claws of Prancer's ribcage became visible. The air scalded with electrostatic screeching and the stench of bergamot. Prancer lay laughing amid the roar of the machinery. The flesh peeled down, revealing his maverick guts like a bloody oyster. Barny saw the whiskered face of the moth emerge from Prancer's navel, a rat abandoning the sinking ship. He snatched the bug into his palm before the belly's evisceration was completed. *I'm a good son after all*, Barny thought, rushing from the terrible room.

That evening in the Swamp of Eternal Enmity/Degradation, Barny watched his parents' shack from the waist-deep concealment of the oozing bog. When the lamps went out, he pushed through the rank smell of leather leaves and waterweeds toward the stained wood of the shack.

Here the swamp was not the most perilous undertow. His roistering but serpent-headed father had chosen to indefinitely postpone acknowledgement of the facts, including that of Barny's genetic relationship to himself. Barny's mother had chosen to do the same – according to each he was the work of the other.

Barny doorcreaked into the shack, where his parents sat asleep in their concrete chairs. The room was illuminated by the dim phosphorescence of Pa Juno's octopal hair, the ghostly glow of which was muted in sleep. The canary cage stood in the far corner, a black mourning cloak covering the cage itself. Barny crept silently over, tipped the fluttering moth carefully from a matchbox and reached it into the cage – it fitted by feel between the bars. Then he turned and instantly stepped on a rope of his father's hair, blasting the house with light and screaming.

'What the hell is your son doing creeping around here?' shouted Pa Juno, squinting through the fog of marriage.

'Ask him – he's your son.'

'Er, look at this,' Barny improvised, spinning back to the cage and flourishing the cloak away. 'It's a miracle.'

On the floor of the cage a fruit bat was flapping one wingtip like blown paper and making small glottal noises, its foxlike face wet-eyed and shutting down.

'What have you done?' shrieked Barny's mother.

'He must have fed it something dry,' hollered Pa Juno.

'Something that wasn't fruit,' whooped Ma Juno. 'After taking our beautiful Ramone from us.'

Barny pointed back at the cage. 'I put this one in his place, didn't I?'

'Did you hear that?' shrieked Ma Juno.

'He'll do the same to us, give him half the chance. Can't you keep your son under control?'

Ma Juno pressed her tear-wet face against the cage bars, toasting her grief. 'I have no son.'

3

Gunpowder Tea

Hoaxers try harder

Gregor, too, had been making progress. Mention of Edgy's name had indeed swung a job at Stampede Products and he was asked to start right away, since another employee had met an 'untimely end', or so the interviewer said with raised eyebrows and the sort of rueful tone which implied that Gregor could easily guess the details.

Gregor steamed in. On the first day a hundred door-steps were enlivened by his desperation. Stampede's ephemera was aimed at couchbound morons for whom a nervous shudder was the liveliest exercise. Along with horror-wipe boots for the modern world they sold Live Pants, the pants which grow with your philosophy; Damage Tonic, guaranteed to leave you twisted and broken as though after some ill-advised venture; the Toilet Heart, a heart which lay beating in the toilet; the Mice Device, which you placed next to a mouse for thoughtful comparison; Eggs, a new concept in noses; Armaggedon Goodies, some bones; and the Impulse Buy, a beautifully packaged object which nobody could ever describe or remember.

Gregor's pitch began well due to his looking fat and

bulby through door peepholes and looking exactly the same when people opened the door. Potential customers laughed a lot and assumed he was a joke telegram. Gregor would chuckle along with them and launch into his spiel. 'If you were an animal, sir, which animal would you be?'

'Eh? Well I am an animal. I'm a human.'

'I mean if you weren't human, what would you be?'

'You think I'm not human?'

'It's just a game.'

'Not to me it isn't. I'm damn proud.'

'And so you should be. As Bingo Violaine said, "Duty enhances the handsome man, is an added burden to the unloved." May I come in? There we are. May I ask, sir, do you exercise?'

'I puff, I puff, it's the same as jogging. And every two weeks I have a kind of hernia, which must be normal.'

'No need with these. Dangerous copper pants. They conduct.'

'What?'

'Electricity. You'll be convulsing, jumping all over. You'll break blood vessels in your head.'

'Is that good?'

'I can guess how it would be,' Gregor nodded, smiling slyly as though at a shared, scampish secret.

The client responded with a sudden facial grimace which could mean almost anything, then the seizing of Gregor by the throat. Whenever something like this happened and Gregor asked what the fella was doing, the reply would be 'Something I should have done a long time ago' or occasionally 'What anyone would do'. It got to the point where Gregor would pipe, 'Don't tell me,' and chant the remark before them.

His favourite product was the Stampede Socket Truss. The prolonged haranguing which accompanied it was a masterpiece of what marketeers call the 'assumptive'.

'The Stampede Socket Truss is able to accomplish what no other eye-truss can.'

'What?'

'I'm glad you asked me. Stampede have designed the Socket Truss to lift and separate the eyes without tugging them out of the sockets. No more cracks from the mother-in-law about you having eyes too close together like a drooling pervert. No more people yelling at, yes, you sir in the street, calling you an inbred cracker water-brain with a forehead a small boy could use for stunt-boarding. Shall I put you down for fifty trusses or the full hundred?'

At this point the client would eject him in a sudden frenzy of discrimination. The only person who expressed any interest in the socket truss was Max Gaffer, who believed it was an article of underwear. When the lawyer realised his mistake and went to close the door on him, Gregor insisted too late that it could be used for that as well. Copious use of the word 'myriad' and 'uses' in his bellowed spiel failed to unseal the door. He forgot to even mention the Live Pants.

Toward the end of the day he rang at a door which opened to reveal a small wedge-headed dingbat with knitting-needle antennae and dense pin teeth. All jaw and claw and gleeful prancing, it chittered instant inter-est in the Levity Closet and the Death Challenge Kettle. It was the same demon that had appeared to him under the tree the other night. Gregor tore himself away from the sure sale and ran as fast as his arms and legs could take him.

Gregor felt deflated. Following Barny's advice re the Church of Automata, he visited the Grand Dollimo at their pipe-filigreed factory and claimed he was at the end of his tether. The Dollimo, sitting behind a hydraulic desk, steepled his gloved hands. He was masked in a business suit, bowler and smoked-glass face. 'You echo with dominoes,' he decided, 'all those clinking dogmas. You need merely choose one and the noise ends. I could help you. Death must battle all the more for the practical man. Fit your fancies to my twisted will this instant. Without a doubt, you will gain the joy of feeling specific.'

'Sounds perfect,' blurted Gregor without comprehension.

'Come this way – I'll give you but a glimpse of the dummyworks, accountable to no one.

'This crane has a lifting power of three hundred tons,' shouted the Dollimo above the roar of dynamos in the turbine hall. 'Ahead is a thousand-horsepower drive platform. Face gripping is a relatively simple mechanism.'

'Glad to hear it.'

'Culture life and put it in plastic heads, gag as it restarts.'

Gregor glimpsed creepy marionettes and toddling dolls on the slurry floor below. Periodically these hinge babies disappeared into the sprocket-barnacled walls. Floor lobsters collided and scuttled over each other.

The Dollimo remarked upon assorted doll ordnance as they descended a stairwell near the main forge. It was all hammering diesels and steaming boilerplates, none of it connecting with Gregor's problems. 'Thanks, Grand Dollimo, this is a good facility, thanks for letting me look.'

As they re-entered the office the Dollimo turned to regard him. 'You seem uncommitted.'

Gregor realised vinyl people were watching silent and jewel-eyed, encased in the shelving. He backed carefully through his own bullshit. 'But how does this stuff help with the blood clock?'

The unnatural sheen of the Dollimo's glass mask was point-blank in Gregor's face. 'The blood clock.'

'In the town square. The mechanical knights, that's why I'm here – I can't stop thinking about the blue one. They're automata, aren't they?'

'It becomes clear to me,' said the Dollimo without inflection, 'that your life is an unsavoury mess of indulgence and demonism. A figure needs three or more moving parts to qualify as an automaton. Amateur. You waste my time.'

'But they're hinged, they're made of wood,' Gregor bawled as the Dollimo directed him from the room. Gloss-faced mannequins were clappering with laughter.

'Take it outside, you freak.'

Tired and wretched, Gregor wandered through the Square, halting briefly before the mayoral palace. He looked up at the blood clock, its descending array of bowls and gutters through which the liquid was tilted, slowly displacing weight to tip the gears into motion. The red-gold doors were closed, the hour not at hand. Gregor reminded himself of the words of the philosopher Violaine: 'Wounds close without fanfare.'

'Plenty more fish in the sea,' Gregor hummed, 'and they all hate me.' Forever loyal to his reputation as a bloated fool who persevered, he went across town toward the Powderhouse, his steps lagging, head beginning to droop, until he arrived at the thick door all lumpen and hopeless. This was the only other religion he knew around here and he might as well give it a try. He thumped his head against the door.

The door nudged open. 'Waterproof Integrity Grits,' Gregor said with a quaver in his voice. 'A meal in itself.' He displayed the product gingerly.

A fusehead, confetti in his hair and a slight smirk quirking the corner of his mouth, examined Gregor and seemed to decide. 'Face-first we go, nonstop and altogether. Observe our duties.'

Gregor was ushered into a monstrous chamber rico-cheting with supplicants. Pop-streamers splurted and fell over fuseheads eating rocket salad and riding an onyx jackass. With sporadic yelps these guys were springing pell-mell past bronze sconces and windows of blue rose glass. A few agile mutants swung off the fittings, all frivolity and ostentation. Even the grubs were wearing bikinis.

This was more like it, thought Gregor. People bouncing over and living for the instant like dogs.

'I am instructed to dither and be minimal,' said the fusehead who had opened the door, 'until you look for someone who will use their brain.'

Cannonites in blast regalia lined up to welcome Gregor as he passed.

'I perform the jelly services. Making sure a body can be ignored and dry. Clasped and bundled.'

'I'm the Neck Minister. Ensuring no air or saliva persists in the throat. It's prestigious, in its way. Some necks are thick. Some old. I've knotted cord around them all.'

'I undermine you and open your bags.'

Another handed him a laminated card. 'Death-rattle guidelines.'

'And who is this pork being?'

These words were addressed to the temple at large by a lank, exhausted jester in black and blue, his every gesture one of bemused satiation. He leant negligently, over-casually against an ornamental cannon of jade and gold. 'He has the look of a man who committed a few tentative misdemeanours and then ran like an egg. Come nearer where I can ignore you.'

Gregor shuffled forward. 'Are you . . . Rod Jayrod?'

Fanning himself with a fern, Jayrod met his gaze blandly. 'Just try and stop me.'

'I'm a salesman,' Gregor stammered, raising the produce.

'A dainty predicament,' said Jayrod, looking without interest at the Fainting Cannibal Commemorative Plates. 'Almost too dainty to live long. And you've ears like deformed tubers, I see. Well, your inconvenient fancies and first-class drolleries are not welcome here.'

Gregor frowned up at the cage dancers and the swirling cannonical ideograms in the sweating blast walls. Flaring in firelight were stone sentinels with neck and limbs elongated as though cartoonishly zooming.

'Those fancy cornices won't save you, pig man – nor your comely bewilderment. Luckily I am so weary with satiation I seek recourse in talking to you, a bloke whose head is no particular shape. It's not all bad. Should we find that you're a real delight, the prospects are practically limitless.'

Gregor considered that the chances of anyone finding him 'a real delight' were poor and getting poorer. 'Thank you, er . . . Fusemaster? I'm sorry I don't know the formalities, I just popped into the other place across town and they chased me out of there.'

'The so-called Church of Automata?' trumpeted Jayrod. 'Those simulacra of theirs contaminate everything with their scary games and waddling. Threw you out, did they? A point in your favour. So you roll up here, spoiling for enlightenment. My advice for life is, get out the way of the rolling gong.' With an easy smile the lurid layabout pushed himself from his resting place and took Gregor by the arm. 'In the Cannon Sect our procedures are primarily funerary. More round than a circle, the cannonball leads the way. Until then, we make it a point to thrive like bastards. This inordinate revelry keeps our powder dry. We skip through meadows of magenta reprimand. And when our time comes the Gospel makes plain the escape

31

velocity, burst index and trajectory required to send us speeding out of this poor world. There is written the ready reckoner of body weights and powder charge, the glory of the blur. Immortal? I don't want to still be alive when they're stacking chairs. Do you feel it, pig man? Double negatives are a no-no.'

Feeling warm with conviction, Gregor jumped. 'I guess I do. I guess I'm in.'

'Whatever you like, I'll need your signature here, here and . . . here.'

'Your chin? Your eye?'

'And my arse, that's right. We'll make a man of you. Or something. Here are the Powder Protocols. Learn well this incomprehensible gibberish. It's all there – chapter and verse. Now come this way, whatever your name is.'

Before tall black curtains at the rear of the temple lay a low shrine of blue gemstone into which the form of some object had been pressed as though into dental resin. 'Here resided our holy relic the Wesley Kern gun, until it was plundered from us – one day it will be restored and the culprit found fatally wounded and twitching in a turnip field.' The languid riddler gestured to a baby on stilts, who pulled on a rope – the curtains floated apart to reveal the titanic metal image of the revellers' cannon-mouthed godhead. Dead eyes of blue gold regarded Gregor. 'Isn't she a beauty? The slow smoke out of those urns gives it a doomy feel. The Powdermouth belches on the hour, purifying us all. Supplication here is something I cannot recommend sufficiently. Take your time.'

Gregor stepped uncertainly toward the steaming god-head, his caution yet to catch up with the evening's turn of events. Be slow and large, said Violaine – they'll accommodate.

Gregor cleared his throat and looked up into the giant

face. 'Birds,' he said. 'They vamoose through the air, why?'

'I don't know what the deal is with that,' said a voice from the black oven of the god's mouth.

All activity ceased in the temple. The iron expression had become a strangeness surrounded by prayer eyes and awful silence. Forested faces looked pale and undone. Rod Jayrod let the fern slip from his hand.

Gregor wasn't sure if this was usual. 'You said?'

'You, pig man,' came the reverberative voice from the round, smoky maw, 'you I have chosen. Yes, Round One, this tinpot god smiles upon you like a barber upon his victim, thank you yes. Give me a minute to think and I'll dispense your chores.'

'Chores? Well, I've already got to learn this rubbish.' Gregor raised the Powder Protocols.

'Bring your friends through the creepchannel direct to your god, and they will have jelly and ice cream.'

'What flavour?'

'Do not question your god, pig man. And the trip must be a surprise for all, especially Barny Juno, who pleases me greatly thank you sir.'

'I prefer to remain, er . . . aloof from mortal danger. Coquettish, mysterious. I run and giggle, all that.'

But Gregor was already being swept up by the revellers and hailed a 'Holy One'. A banger went off in his eye.

Amid the chaos the cannon mouth fired and nobody saw Skittermite flying, all arms and legs, through the air to splat against the main doors.

Around this time Prancer Diego set fire to his arse in the town square and shoved away those who came to help him. 'Adapt to new surprises, naughty boy! Immortal superiors are on the screen and even worms are despairing! I'm outta me head with this blood-drinking, boss –

the land's completely random!' And Prancer embarked on a high-kneed capering dance for no reason and in utter silence. 'I'm excellent and show it, so what? In this pantleg's a leg, in this one's a heavy heart.'

Passers-by bellied up, indignant. 'Shut up, crazy man.'

'Could you optimise the bribe so I can afford new clothes?'

'Bribe?' shouted a thug by the name of GI Bill. 'We're having a fistfight.'

'A fistfight? I wanna spell it out like this – e-t-e-r-n-i-t-y.'

'You can spell it any way you want, but we're gonna fight.'

'Will you save me?'

'What? We're gonna fight, you goddamn fool.'

'I'm a chimpanzee, look – ha ha!'

'Keep still you sonofabitch—'

'I can't, I'm excited!'

GI Bill retreated with his face a riot of disgust.

'Letters taste like dandelions!' Prancer shrieked. 'Take me home daddy! Even as you look I smash the standard!' Prancer claimed to have found life insurance papers in the baby-pouch of a badger. He produced a jagged scroll which appeared to have been cut from human skin. 'Read and weep, my friends.' He clunked to his knees, sobbing like a castaway. 'Weep for the deadly boy I was.'

The scroll began with a blurred purple heading, *The Cyril Manifesto*.

4

Attaboy, Mike

Untended, questions grow wild

When Barny told Magenta Blaze about the dead bat she laughed like a drain and urged him to do the same. Their relationship was conducted amid a saturation-bombing of misunderstandings and strenuous suspension sex. Now they sat in the Ultimatum Restaurant, where Barny had once again been required to eat some kind of bony, barbed flail. The alternative had been pasta.

Magenta cast a pink shadow, her heart full of crossed wires.

'I killed him,' Barny wept. 'It's doing my nut in.'

'He went to heaven,' Magenta laughed. 'That's what you always say.'

'I know.' Barny blew his nose on a petition for his death which remained from a past débâcle. Realising what it was, he threw it aside before Magenta could see. She had him solidly pegged as a wild and colourful man and he didn't want to remind her of this occasion. As they entered the restaurant he had noticed the front of the establishment was newly sprayed with the slogan CYRIL IS LOVELY. Barny had no idea what it meant but he rushed her past it anyway, fearing that by some obscure route even this scrawl might enhance his prowess in her eyes. 'Anyway, I've got something to tell you. I didn't want you to hear it from someone else.'

'This sounds mysterious,' said Magenta, hunkering down for intrigue.

'No, no,' Barny moaned wearily, 'nothing's mysterious, it's boring, I'm boring and completely uneventful.'

'Bubba, you are funny. What about that fight you had in the Shop of a Thousand Spiders?'

'That's because Edgy tore someone's shirt. He dragged me in there – I don't even enjoy the place. I don't really like going out at all. I'm not very social, I hardly ever laugh, I don't like excitement. I just want to take care of the winged and stepping animals of the earth.'

Cake-pale between hoop earrings, Magenta's face was blank.

'Know what I mean?'

Realisation dawning, Magenta became embarrassingly giddy. 'You killed it deliberately?'

Barny was bewildered. It was hopeless. He gave her a sickly look. What the hell could he do with this girl? Now she was grinning wolfishly for some reason.

Barny started thinking about the Power Shout – what was going on there? He almost never raised his voice much. Gregor whined and ranted, Edgy barked and jittered; Barny didn't even yelp when the leopard clawed his leg.

Maybe the Power Shout was one of those etheric exercises Edgy talked about sometimes. It involved putting the image of an idea into your belly and then breathing out and shooting the idea-molecule at someone. Edgy once used it to trip a mime into a fast-flowing river. The Power Shout was probably that sort of thing, but shouting the idea at the same time.

Barny began revving up. He drew the notion together in his head, bringing it to fine focus. He took a deep breath.

The waiter came to the table. 'More coffee?'

'*WE'RE FINISHED!*' bellowed Barny. The waiter collapsed like a cut puppet.

Barny recovered from his exertion to see Magenta convulsed with laughter. 'Barny, you are *unbeatable*.'

'A drive in the country?'

'Or perish in the attempt.'

Edgy and Gregor were walking across the dusty street toward Dot Spacey's gas station. In exploring lethargy as an artform, Dot had set upon achieving the sunset ideal of 'total immobility'. He sat on the forecourt like a mascot as Mike Abblatia, whose back was giving him increasing pain, ran to please all. 'Welcome, Mr Gregor – I got the car ready.'

'Say no more about it,' Gregor laughed nervously. He had asked Abblatia to soup up a vehicle for creepchannel travel. Scarcars were so rare and expensive that few believed they existed. As Abblatia chugged the buggy from around the side of the garage, the sun glared on bony spars, scapula spoilers and tyre radials of human flesh.

'The hood's black for void mergence,' said Mike Abblatia, getting out to raise it and tinker with the engine. Gregor and Edgy watched with rueful fascination as he ratcheted cytoma and spritzed the fatty meat of the cylinder head. 'Vertebral shocks. Heavy duty.'

'You don't need to tell *us*,' Gregor urged him with a forced smile. His god-commanded task had beguiled that part of his mind which would normally build a sandwich. There was little room for anything else. But the car was clearly giving Edgy pause for thought. Gregor acted brisk and hearty. 'It's the only car he had available. Okay, let's go.'

'So, are you guys gonna pay now?'

'Don't worry, Mike,' Edgy sniggered, and he slapped Abblatia on his swollen back. 'Remember what old Bingo said. "Hunches are coordinates from a different angle."'

They piled in and were about to leave when they felt a rhythmic shoving at the car – looking back, they saw that Dot Spacey had stood and was indulging in sexual congress with the gas tank. They had both forgotten about this tradition. It went on for a while, the two men sitting in silence as the car jiggled from side to side.

'Boy, it's hot,' said Edgy after a while.

'Yeah. There's a ladybird on the windscreen.'

'Well, maybe we won't need it.'

'What's that stuff they use?' asked Gregor, making a wiping motion.

'Turtle wax.'

'Huh. What a life.'

The car stopped moving. Mike Abblatia appeared at the window. 'He's finished,' he called, giving them the thumbs-up.

'Sweet as granny biscuits,' said Gregor with relief, and they pulled out in a cloud of red flake dust.

A couple of torturers approached Sweeney's living armoured throne. They were simplistic, rotund demi-demons with big eyes. 'We've made rapid progress in the torture chamber.'

'Discarded limbs crackling in the grate?'

'Better than that. We've been growing roses.'

'I beg your pardon.'

'Oh yes – their satin finery is a crazy marvel.'

Sweeney leaned forward in strenuous scrutiny, aghast. 'Their "satin finery" belongs in cages! Are you blurred in the head? Roses! A cheap conjuring trick!'

'Oh, no – not those beauties surely. Does it hurt anyone?'

'Exactly – does it?'

'Oh, lighten up, Master.'

'Lighten up? What's that you're holding?'

'An apple.'

'You're eating an apple?'

'I'm about to.'

'Oh no you're bloody not, Sonny Jim.' The braided roots of Sweeney's brain began arcing from his skull seams like worms in a rainstorm. 'Don't you understand we're managing an open-ended apocalypse here? Rich hours of ingenuity, succulent little abominations. Not apples, not roses. Easy meat gurgling open. Life's puzzle is only as deep as their body – it's down to us to scatter the pieces.' He stared at them. 'You don't know what I'm talking about, do you? Oh hell – I free your lesson!'

Darkness peeled off the wall and began spinning fast, wrapping around the two demi-demons. As they blurred, flaying into shavings of glass and sawdust, Sweeney considered a torture befitting Juno. Those above needed something graphic. Confronted with the hollowed head of their best, they'd cave.

Barny and the gorgeous Chloe Low were admiring a couple of ghoulish statues in Scardummy Garden when the replicas exploded like dandelion heads, showering them with sand. 'That's nothing,' coughed Chloe, slapping the dust from her clothes, shaking it from her blue-black hair. 'Look at this one.' She pointed out other fierce constructs in the tangled bushes around the precinct's edges. The Garden contained a statue of each and every Accomplice citizen and it was traditional to deck and groom your own during a visit. But Barny had never seen these tombyard beasts before, clasped and blended as they were into greenery. Something like an ankled rope of bones hunched toward the sky. A bat skeleton the size of a child crouched over a broken bottle. A hat and coat with scythe arms stood serene and ready. A thug of scraps grinned, all cheek and snot. A winged knight with a head like a tomahawk – this last Barny did recognise. 'That's Dietrich Hammerwire,' said Chloe, a nice notch in her brow. 'It's a mega paravamp, a draco-class demon. Strange that they're all here, isn't it? Part of the community.'

Certain minutes are like a doughnut, the very thing. Sitting on a bare plinth, Chloe gazed at toppled pillars, drifting air silk and world light. A tree whisked around, Barny's dog Help capered near a basilisk platform, earth rust was baked by the sun. Here was a bush before the wind, the drained blue table under the wall, the bottomless sky, and amazing silence. And Barny was gazing bovine at Chloe, her smile longer by inches; watching the girl shift buttocks and squint at the sky. In this strange corpse orchard, a vast plain of pillared people, his heart ripened and peached.

'Lessons settle like a new grave and we're quiet,' Chloe whispered. 'A simple insect grudge match can be perfect. All my resources squeal to a halt here. I can lay down and get busy with the sky.' She turned on to her back. 'Before he fired from the Tower, one of the things Wesley Kern asked for was a siesta.'

'What's that?'

'A sleeping time in the afternoon. It wasn't always this warm here, Barny. But when the weather changed, employers didn't want to accept the traditions of hotter places. Working hours were the longest in the world.'

'A siesta,' said Barny thoughtfully, noticing a weed-grown flagstone sprayed with the red words NICE CYRIL. 'People should sleep whenever they want, like other animals.'

'That's what he said. And the Mayor dismissed the idea despite sending everyone to sleep with speeches. Kern paid a servant to belt the Mayor around the head every afternoon and photograph the inert body next to a clock. With these images he produced a set of fifty collector's cards and schoolkids fiended to amass them all. The rarest was number seventeen, in which the Mayor's gob was stuffed with a half-eaten pineapple – only one copy of the card had been produced. When the Mayor was stuck for campaign funds, Kern gave him card seventeen and the Mayor's advisers confirmed he could sell it at auction for thousands. The indignity of that auction left the Mayor in a bathroom alone, weeping like an ice sculpture. At exactly the same time that Kern himself was killed by doves, the local shaman seemed to evaporate. Only his earlobes were left, looking like squeezes of dough. Then someone with more money than sense put them in a bell jar and encouraged them to mate. Bedded down in angel cress, they'd soon spread like a bead curtain. After several weeks the earlobes resembled a pale honeycomb. A document in the Juice Museum says this growth eventually became the current shaman, Beltane Carom. I sometimes think about that. Remember what Violaine said: *Do you think the past is contained within the present? The past has escaped to its own freedom and doesn't think of us.*'

Chewing a sandwich, Barny nodded without meaning or comprehension. Chloe put him to shame once a week with mindbogglers from the Juice Museum, a treasure-house of denied facts and bricked histories. Barny contented himself with the headswim of staring but his friend Mr Peterson, the nearest thing he had to a functioning father figure, warned him that if he didn't take a lead she'd kick his heart into the long grass. 'We know women have control over men; we assume they have control over themselves. What else, Bubba?' But when Barny looked at Chloe Low, something came loose in him. And what about Magenta? She would not accept him as he was. Now Chloe was talking about an archive of doors in the Juice Museum. These doors had been pulled from their jambs in such a way that some of the space behind them had come away too, like a tap root.

Barny mawed his mouth, crumbs falling. 'Chloe, er . . .'

A car screeched up in the lane on the other side of the hedge and Edgy's tufted head appeared. 'Pile in, Boo, we're goin' on a picnic.'

They went and peered over the bush. 'We're on one already,' said Barny. 'Where'd you get this flashy motor?'

'Stole it from good old Mike Abblatia. He's a helluva guy. We're having jelly and ice cream. Sorry, Low – only room for one.'

Barny scarfed up the rest of the sandwich and piled in, the dog Help leaping in after him.

Chloe flapped her arms against her hips. 'Well, all right, 'bye.'

'See you outstretched on the cake then,' shouted Edgy as they roared off.

What have I done? thought Barny as strange, unhinged laughter exploded around him. Edgy, Fang and Sags Dumbar from the office were here, and Gregor was driving without joy, sweating like a bastard. Barny wished he could think fast, like a housefly.

'Hey,' called Edgy, 'you and Prancer are doing a great job hoaxing the Cyril thing, Bubba.'

'What are you talking about?'

'He told me all about it, collaborating on the Manifesto? Boy, that's a wild read.'

Above the roar of the drive Gregor seemed to be saying stuff about the cannon church – the same one Barny had annoyed once by burying a lizard. 'Yeah, it's quite a scene over there. Quite a scene.'

One minute they were ploughing through some financial advisers in a field, then the car gave a booming cough as it dropped into a yellow intensity of spinelight and etheric corrosion. Bodies tensed with distress and full recognition of the situation's novelty value as magnetism bent the air and they shot down the channel like a guillotine blade. The car was a fluorescent smear tearing through taut skeins of migraine aura. The spaniel had his head out the window, a smile on his face as slams of turbulence sailed his ears and black glitter blasted by. Bile bugs were drumming across the roof.

The channel spiralled and Barny looked aside at Sags Dumbar, whose strange aqueous head was glowing like a shaded lamp – sickstone ribs and antique cannolis rushed past, mildly refracted through the transparency. 'I'll have the roast beef platter,' Sags remarked. They smashed through a glass alarm and into a sofa made of bread – contempt barged these trifles aside, trailing lightning-like sparks. Brain vapour was glincing the windshield and the atmosphere swarmed with urgent repairs.

Then they seemed to hover, venting exhaust. Barny looked out the window – they were atop a rolling red boulder, coasting in the arsenic light of a channel junction. Edgy's screams were so notoriously insightful that people sought him out to inflict some agony – now he outdid himself, yelling at Gregor to strip the gears if he had to. Cranking, Gregor gunned the motor and they tore away from the king corpuscle, down an arcade of wounds in a cold, screaming rush. The gas tank exploded, herbal soup stains flaying back at the windshield.

Counting the petals of a larkspur in preparation for the 'loves me/loves me not' game, Magenta Blaze strode down Owl Transfer Street. Was Barny being truthful or just filling out some quota of self-effacement? Antisocial, never goes out, never laughs, avoids excitement? Surprising herself, she decided to put aside any possible prejudice and take a chill look at the facts.

Ahead of her, a ribcaged car exploded through the display window of the Shop of a Thousand Spiders in a garish spray of interface medicine, dreamspore, thaumaturgical artefacts and activans. Baulking to a halt and standing in a slow leak of benthic steam, the car stood striped with crash tar, a rear bumper sticker reading I BRAKE FOR HADES. The bodywork had acquired a dark coating of burnt nerve tissue and now cracked open, muffled hilarity turning fully audible as a door bust to earth with Barny upon it, weeping with laughter. Everyone piled out, gobs distorted by speed and dementia. 'Wow that was so cool,' said Fang. Edgy seemed to find his remark hilarious. Everyone's chin had been converted temporarily to dense, fibrous wood, and they began clacking these like hanging puppets. The dog Help yapped and skipped around.

Satisfied that Barny and his friends were a healthy crew, roistering with youthful humour and camaraderie, Magenta turned and crept the other way.

Dietrich stormed into the cavern after stewing for hours. 'With respect, Majesty. Kermit doesn't know how bloody random it is up there. He's just a vex. He won't be able to navigate.'

Sweeney, throned in poison plenty, was unimpressed. 'Who do you suggest, if not a pestilent?'

'Trubshaw, Rakeman, Feroce. Anything's better than some latchkey fiend who thinks it's clever to walk on his buttocks. Those people up there'll absently kick his bones off the front step. I tell you, the world proceeds without them as they attend to other matters.'

'In true terms even you're wet behind the wings,

Dietrich. Why enter the game to end it? The continual efforts of the harmless damned entertain us. Let's view Skitter's progress.'

Sweeney called down the Aspict. As the dark red revulsion diamond lowered into view, it became clear it was not in tip-top condition. Its light was clouded, the vermiform innards totally obscured.

Belted radial tyre-marks crisscrossed the surface. Sweeney's eye on the upper realm was blinded.

5

Presume Zone

Blood can't be counted

The Mayor was shaken and embarrassed that the Cyril movement was manifesting in objective reality. Stupid slogans were appearing everywhere and the square had been blessed with a 'speaking truncheon' which passers-by approached tentatively. The Mayor watched from his office window as a citizen touched the black missile and incited a stream of incendiary abuse which scattered everyone amid shrieks. 'It's a sort of miracle, I suppose,' he said dismally, and turned to see Max Gaffer smile at the absurd lie. 'Very well, I wish it wasn't there. In a very real way. No speaking truncheons in the town square, that's my motto. That way, the most authority has to grapple with is normal human disinterest. We'll issue a pamphlet.'

Gaffer winced. There was a famously inaccurate pamphlet issued by the Mayor's office which stated that 'all dead birds explode eventually. Love it or loathe it, you can't change nature.' The pamphlet, entitled 'Am I Safe From Birds?', did offer some useful guidelines on dove attacks, dove insurance and dove evasion, this last under the sub-heading 'Any Fool Can Dodge Doves'.

There was a small cartoon of the Mayor himself, his expression making it clear he was not to be trifled with, springing over a garden pond. The last page bore the image of a placid swan and the slogan BUTTER WOULDN'T MELT. The Mayor had had some explaining to do when he demonstrated his ideas by dressing a servant as the devil and spearing him to death on the balcony. 'No more fatal stabbings during speech!' he had noted in his journal, underlining the reminder three times. The only successful pamphlet the Mayor had ordered was about skybikes, terrifying stained-glass penny farthings driven silently in circles by skeletons in the night sky. The pamphlet, called 'Don't Be Scared of Skybikes', assured the public that these aerial apparitions were an omen of good luck, and that the Mayor himself invited such phantom visitations with puckering lips. After the booklet had been distributed, thirty-six skybikes collided in the air above the mayoral palace at four in the morning, spattering the roof with neon bones and other ectoplasmic shite.

'You'd better take a look at this, sir.' Gaffer handed over a sheet of paper. 'They're turning up everywhere, even in my pants.'

'What nonsense is this? The "Cyril Manifesto"?' He scanned it quickly, his face congested:

You're exposed to a mob of friends so you'll worry. Then a towel is put to use on your ears, and a photograph is taken. Finally you're burnt in effigy on a traffic island. But the real you – boy oh boy. You'll glower till they laugh. Approach the raindrops with a length of string. Dash across the graveyard with a surfboard. Brandish sausages at a weeping old man. Telephone the opera and mention a hen. That's got to light up your considerations, hasn't it?

The Mayor was appalled. 'This is disastrous. How can anyone see Cyril as a proper nemesis when its credo has been composed by cattle?'

'The problem is,' said the lawyer, 'that it's proving popular. Cyril meetings are springing up everywhere.'

'What? But the ideas are shockingly arbitrary. This thing's been blown out of someone's nose. Beguiling minutes I spent believing that it made sense. Then the realisation, and the anger.'

'Remind you of anyone?'

'Eh? Not . . . Turbot, you mean? My own speech writer?'

'Noam B. Turbot. He's done worse. Booting the focus groups, remember? Blundered in here with a stolen nest in one hand and a roulette wheel in the other. Knee-walking drunk. We haven't enough binoculars to make that man a giant.'

Disturbed, the Mayor half-fell into the nearest chair. 'Beware the reviving scrape of God's claw, that's what Violaine said wasn't it? Well, whoever's responsible, this idle malice could wreck everything. And the Conglomerate? They'll have my arse for a throwrug. We're too far along to devise a different public outcry. For a while I'm their liberator. We'll look back at this as the time of purchase, the joke fresh. What to do. We should ideally keep our legs busy while thinking this over. Even I take a stroll occasionally and I'm quite burly. If it weren't for these bloody floor lobsters.' He kicked one like a toy – it scudded a short way across the carpet and halted, unharmed.

'Perhaps we could sell these notional roaches as food for the poor,' the lawyer suggested lightly.

'Yes,' the Mayor muttered thoughtfully. 'Yes, see to it – and sweeten the deal with a few miniature swine made of pyrex. Everyone loves a pig, a small one of that kind. It's a sad turn of affairs but in politics you learn to cry with your ears – nobody's expecting that. Not in a million years.'

'Outstanding, sir. And the manifesto?'

'There's information in a hoax. Enough maybe to reverse into the perpetrator. Go see Turbot, then maybe we'll attend one of these little meetings. It is indeed a tragedy on the street when acid words effect democracy, eh?'

Gregor had failed and it was like he'd shaken off half a hypnosis. Did it matter so much what the Powdermouth said? A few days ago he'd barely heard of the thing.

But the car trip had bonded him again with Barny and the crew – they'd slapped him on the back so many times he coughed up some lamb he'd eaten earlier. And now Edgy insisted on putting him up at the Bata Motel, where he maintained occupancy by pretending to be a ghost. 'Rotten glass and fire map on the door, etc,' said Edgy, throwing his keys on the side table and opening the fridge. 'Anything dreadful in this room is yours.'

'Thank you, Plantin. Where's the bathroom?'

'Wherever you like. If the maintenance guy comes up unexpectedly, just beat hell out of him.'

'Beat hell out of the maintenance guy,' repeated Gregor, nodding.

Edgy was a practitioner of fridge meditation, that moment of blank reverie which occurs upon opening the fridge and forgetting why. Gregor waited respectfully while Edgy communed with the milky glow.

Presently Edgy threw the door closed and Gregor gave him a quick smile. 'I couldn't help but notice you've got a gravestone in here.'

'Oh, this is the royal jelly of frighteners,' Edgy stated, patting the gravestone like a dog. 'This little baby's pulled my chestnuts out of the fire so many times. I just move it around every day, so if anyone comes in, it's in a different position and gives 'em the first-rate heeby-jeebies. Then I create the illusion of a ghost like the fumes from a tyre fire, by setting fire to some tyres.' Edgy chuckled. 'And I bought a cormafester in the Thousand Spiders.' Edgy indicated a crablike medallion over the door, black and throbbing. 'One of those weird house growths nobody dares examine or walk under. So dense it's guaranteed to give everyone the fear. There's yellow jelly in the fire hydrant. And a gutted betsy lamp at the window, harmless really but looks ominous. Oh, by the way, the old goat who runs the Shop of a Thousand Spiders, she's not too happy about you using the creepchannel exit at the back of the store.'

'I didn't know it was there. I mean I didn't remember – we just got spat out there by the luck of the draw. So listen, when did this whole ghost thing start?'

'A year ago. Had an argument with the landlady. My rent was in arrears.'

'Why put it in her ears?'

'Arrears – listen to what I'm saying, Round One.'

'So you muffled them with your rent money? What's the *matter* with you?'

Edgy shrugged on a new Hawaiian shirt. 'Well, it's the phone. The engaged recording keeps telling me to replace the receiver, so I do. It's costing me a fortune buying those things. Anyway, unshaven and into the fray, I knew my bills would remain unpaid. Then I hit on this little ghost number. Only problem is the sound through the floorboards. In fact I got an idea for Stampede Products – soundproof carpet. You can stamp, drop stuff, fall over.' Edgy giggled, chuffed. 'And nobody'll be any the wiser. So how's it going at Stampede?'

'Good. And they think I could work in the autumn, as a sort of lost man standing around.'

'That's what you do all year.'

Gregor sat on the bed. 'Well, they saw that and were illuminated.'

Edgy popped a beer and scrutinised Gregor. 'So what's the score with this baggy-pants farce you call a religion, Round One? How did it happen?'

'I don't know, I just blundered in there and the next thing I knew, I was being told to read up on all this stuff. That Powdermouth statue's a beauty, though – like I was saying to Barny, it fires gas and effluvia from its gob every hour on the hour. I think that's the rumble we feel around then. They gave me this novice fuse to wear, some devotional gunpowder. They think I'm some kind of special person.'

'Oh, they probably say that to everyone. Those high-kicking cultists'll give you more famous church scratches than you can possibly follow. What you got there?'

Gregor frilled the sacred volume without enthusiasm. 'Velocity Gospel. I have to learn the Powder Protocols, Chip's Strife Angle Theory, ascension telemetry, the Ballistic Catechism, a Murphy One curse, Deloquatant's Sin and the first five platitudes. The catechism's all questions and answers like "When a man blurs, does he cease to exist?"'

'So what's the answer?'

'No.'

'Oh, Round One, Round One, why waste your time? I don't like to see you like this, all pumped up on support mechanisms and meaning.'

'But it admits in the introduction, "It is in the nature of the document that darkness and irritation impacts in flashes."'

'As a friend, Round One, I've gotta tell you Barny may be a little simple-minded but you're downright weak.

Well it's your life, it's your time, but me, I don't like churches. Cutlery chain on the truth, or they'd like you to think so. Doll worship's the same; and anyway that Dollimo and Distaff frighten the life outta me. And by the way, do you know this cannon church of yours came about by mistake?' Edgy was lalloping back and forth, gesturing with the can as he declaimed. 'Too much fuel in the crematorium. Massive blast, you know. Coffin fired half a mile in the air. So here they are blasting bodies into the stratosphere and plastering the act with terminology. Between you and me, Round One, I once crashed one of their affairs at a funeral switching yard. "Chap with earlobe," I lied, "came to pay my respects." "We all have earlobes here," they said. "Then I'll feel right at home," I said. "You wish to enter through discord?" they said. "Damn right I do," I said, and was admitted into a carnival of horrors. They had things called "strutting procedures", where all the strutting they'd denied in the rest of their life was compressed into two minutes of jerky mayhem. And did you ever see a cannon confessional? It's like a gameshow, they dump slime on you, it's terrible. And then the firing itself, pell-mell out the business end of a cannon.' Edgy sat down on the headstone, spent. 'I'm telling ya, Round One. In the graveyard, accidents petition our respect.' He swigged the beer.

Gregor leafed through the book and there, sure enough, was a section which explained 'Quantum Strutting': 'Only with gunpowder in his eyes does a man reflect upon the forces which have used him. Strut, strut, strut.' In his head Gregor heard the reverberative squawk of the Powdermouth. Had he been distracted? Wasn't there something else personal he should be dealing with about now?

Putting the book aside, Gregor urged Edgy to continue his haunting instructions. Edgy based his teaching methods on those of his own ear-laughter tutor – he had been attending lessons in the art for two and a half years, and he took it very seriously. He could now snicker quietly through his ears and was assured he would be able to guffaw within a few months. 'It's way more advanced than ear-crying,' Edgy snorted. 'Everyone does that.'

'But the one thing I don't get,' said Gregory, 'is what we do if the landlady comes in.'

Edgy opened a small cupboard. 'We get in there.'

'In there, are you crazy?'

'You know you could go stay at Barny's.'

'I'm scared of the lion and the leopard.'

'Oh, you can never have too many big cats, Round One. Anything else is a false economy.'

Barny charged off the street, through the snout distillery, the flower store, the bar full of angry failures, the sauna, the printshop, the karate school, the giant mouth, the movie theatre, the bowling alley and into the street. 'Dago – so what's the story? You told everyone I wrote some half-arsed manifesto with you? Like I don't have enough trouble caring for the winged and stepping animals of the earth?'

Prancer Diego tore off a wrestler's mask and cawed with laughter. 'Apologies are tools of control, Juniper.'

He pushed a thick wad of leaflets into Barny's pockets. Recognising the duplicated echo of Prancer's stripped flesh, Barny spent a time frowning at one. 'Wait a minute, isn't this complete bollocks? People'll think I'm simple-minded.'

A fiercer bout of hilarity gripped the prankster and shook him like a flag. Tears striped his expression. 'I'll deny it,' he gasped, 'if you do one last thing for me, Juniper.' He produced a camera from a small golden coffin. 'Go look for a face – Cyril needs one. And between us there is a rumbling baboon of a difficulty.'

'What sort of difficulty?'

'My broken lagging. The fridge. The burnt carpet.'

'Carpet?'

'Yes. These all worry me. I can't speak to you directly until these matters are resolved. Push me away.'

'Eh?'

'Push me away now.'

'There.'

'You have. Thank you. My god, I'm glad you understand.'

'I don't understand a damn thing,' Barny began to assert, but where Prancer had stood there was now only a badly assembled scarecrow. Jerky with impatience, Barny dashed the turnip nose from its face and kicked it into the gutter. With a fixed grin, the scarecrow burst into flame. Silky smoke tumbled up from the torso. 'Well.' Barny coughed loudly, utterly baffled and speaking purely for public benefit. 'My work here is done.' And he shuffled away.

The tip of his long downcurving nose having fused with his upturned chin, Noam B. Turbot had reached the age of realising there was no reward. Hair grew from his eyes. There was a good angel on one shoulder and a bad angel on the other, both drunk. He looked out the mossy window, mouth pursed like a fist. 'It's as I suspected. The sun, rising at an angle, has inflicted another morning upon us all.' He shook his head dismally.

'It's near dark,' spat Max Gaffer, entering and halting immediately in disgust at his surroundings. Three floor lobsters tangled with the top of the hat tree. In fact the place was lousy with lobsters. They climbed pillars of smoke-stained timber and among dry bird stuff on the stone mantel. The ceiling fan slewed slow.

Turbot turned from his desk at the window. 'I got your note. Stinking I may be. Great, perhaps. Hell-demon I most certainly am not.'

'The messenger told a tale of violence and reproach.'

'I talk to people so they know it. What's that?' He indicated the leaflet in Gaffer's hand. 'My report card? Must do better?'

'The last speech was a little flowery.'

'Poets are poisonous round the eyes, didn't you know?'

'Poet,' muttered the lawyer, casual and observant. 'So how do you judge this, old man?'

Turbot snatched the manifesto from him and read it in glum silence. 'A failure,' he declared. 'Written, I suspect, by dogs.'

'It calls itself a manifesto.'

'Young dogs, then. It's a myth that revolution isn't fun – there are forged papers, rain, and monologues in the interval. Yes, why not? They're less than powerless. You wish their hatred be diffuse so as not to support violence. Your wish is forever granted.'

'This is the first you've heard about it?' asked the lawyer, examining a flaky lamb skull.

'Meaning what?' asked Turbot, appalled. 'What are you playing at?'

Gaffer's mouth moved in a cool smile. 'An honest man must change as quickly as the rules.'

'You're referring to law-abiders, not honest men.'

'Well, Turbot, you're neither. Not since we picked you out of the chorus. Put you where you are today.' Gaffer examined a framed Violaine motto: *You make more difference to the world emulsioning a wall than you do writing satire.* 'We need another speech, by the way. Portray the manifesto as an unwholesome mind-game.'

'I may, I suppose,' stated Turbot in a pompous voice.

'There are walls in people, sick and essential. Your pretence that you have a choice is understandable.'

Fastidiously distracted, Turbot tapped a moth from the window. 'You forget that it needn't be uncontested. I could offer my services to doomed Eddie Gallo.'

'Oh, please. His faculties come and go according to their own schedule. He'd think you were a daffodil.'

'So regret me. My job is to adapt the presentation of the client's will to the prejudices of the public, so that one is well served and the other feels so for a time. And I suppose you think I'm talking about your underwear?'

'Aren't you?' barked the lawyer.

'Even your bones are superficial, aren't they? Caution the floor, if you want something to do.'

The lawyer drew himself up. He went to the door. 'You're a poor host.'

Turbot sat blandly aloof, eyes almost closed.

'We need the speech tomorrow, old man. Reassure the Conglomerate re your loyalty. It's the smart thing to do.' Gaffer slammed out.

Turbot returned immediately to a fierce scrutiny of the leaflet, his face becoming distorted. This gabble of trash concocted at some punchbowl vigil – its slapdash flare was so galling to him he had been tempted to claim he was the author. In fact he was bitterly flattered that Gaffer had suspected him. How pathetic was that? In such a situation the great Bingo Violaine would have strapped on a set of antlers and pinned Gaffer to the ceiling.

From the beginning Turbot was ill-equipped as a fire-brand – he had had only one item of anger, a poor war chest. The anger hadn't even grown thin with use – he had misplaced it, the worst squander, and it was un-remembered. Reduced to mere maths and ironautics, here he sat, monochrome in old lies. He could pull no more bunnies from his dustbag brain.

Though Bingo Violaine had been drummed out of his body years ago, it was said that he had swerved round the traffic cones of hell's teeth and found himself detached from his own story, persisting as some floating atomic remnant. Turbot hoped vainly that Violaine was looking elsewhere tonight. He was wretched and trivial, owned by others.

He needed the green unheard-of thought that for saps like him occurred only once, in the summer luck of childhood. Where was the juice?

Turbot hefted himself up, stood unsteadily a while, and turned toward the door. 'When a man walks,' he quoted, 'he kicks at his future.'

A night black as old soda, and beneath Barny's eyelids the jelly was giving it all it could. Invisible tabs of sky rolled through his sleep, the outer scuttle of wall lizards translating in dream to the popcorn death of a mime.

Skittermite twitched across the ceiling. Mistaking impatience for initiative, he'd decided to just spring at Barny and claw at his essentials. Looking straight down past haphazard ladders and indoor jetties to the lower floor of Barny's multistorey shack, he saw no movement in the gloom.

Barny's bed was suspended creaking near a platform off the third deck. At the end of the bed a cat sat like a jug, watching Skittermite's spraddle-legged approach without curiosity. But as Skittermite sprang on to one of the guy ropes, the cat gave the slightest miaow and the entire twisted building erupted – shapes on the wall became screaming monkeys, corner shadows swooped in the form of preybirds and the floor stirred with predators. Skittermite fell to the living room in a clot of chimps. Shaggy monsters such as a lion set upon the giblet-jointed tyke, biting at random. Skittermite was scurrying for his life, neon wounds dripping like fluorescent graffiti. The lion loped after him as if it had all the time in the world.

Skittermite climbed a buckled wall toward Barny's bed with a vague plan to beg for help. When he emerged at the bed end, his delta-shaped head a right laugh in the darkness, a blast of light blotted his prehensile eyes. In the after-dazzle, he heard Barny winding on a camera.

6

Drink Me

*Disgrace is one of the classics, requiring a
great number of players*

Skittermite stood in an alleyway, staring up and down the
gallery of posters stamped with his own startled face. The
image bore down on the viewer, maggot-white and
unfocused. The ballpoint nose seemed to be rushing
forward like a spearhead. Underneath hung the slogan:
CYRIL INVENTED CONCERN.

Skittermite had served his time as a novice. Several
months stuck in a drainpipe had taught him the long
view. It had tempered his darting, nervous energy. But
now his brain started to fry. He began to grasp Dietrich's
wary respect for this bandwidth. What was that saying
from Violaine, whose big lower jaw Dietrich kept under
his bed? 'Unnoticed by the target, the strongest dislike
goes into thin air.'

Edgy kept Amy's x-ray tucked in his wallet. She was a
knockout. She wore her veins in a ponytail. After picking
flowers she strapped them to the hood of her car. But she
wanted Edgy to help her publish a book of tormentingly
bad poetry under the title *We Are Taunted on Two
Levels*. She thought he had pull because he had blundered

into the writing of a disastrous book about dogs a while ago. He had included a chapter entitled 'Dogs Which Come Running When a Sergeant Speaks' and this had stuck in the craw zone of the local Brigade. Luckily for Edgy, he had been ghosting the book for Barny Juno and the Brigade focused their vengeful plans on the innocent whose name was on the cover.

'At least change it to *Taunt Us on the Double*,' Edgy told Amy in Snorters Café, his hair in furious condition. 'It's snappier.'

'What?'

'*Taunt Us on the Double*. Eh? Can't you see it? It's a surefire winner, a lock. You're not going to include "I Hate Blue and Love Pigs"?'

'Duh? Of course I'm going to include it. All about how I hate blue and love pigs?' Disgusted, Amy stirred a cup of liquid anxiety.

'Well, what about "The Damned Onions Are Trailing"? Do you have to include that?'

'How could I not?'

'But do you have to call it *We Are Taunted on Two Levels*? Isn't there a way? I'm the one who has to deal with old Testy at the publishers.'

'Listen, mister, if you want to write a book called *Taunt Us on the Double*, that's your right. Mine's called *We Are Taunted on Two Levels*, okay?' Gort swung out of the booth and stormed away.

'Amy!'

As she flashed into the sunlight, crossing the street, Edgy watched her through the window and dreaded a hosepipe ban.

Mayor Rudloe wore a fibreglass containment suit when forced to venture outside – though unwieldy, it kept him from direct contact with the masses. Today it was also protecting him from poisonous gases as he visited the Conglomerate. It was Max Gaffer's first audience with the thing and his first experience of trepidation. 'Grey flowers?' he frowned as they entered the foyer, and the Mayor was uncertain enough to remain silent.

A door opened at the chamber end. The Conglomerate was brimming amid its own uncountable legs. It was wearing a bandmaster's hat. 'That's right – that's right, children, come in, I won't bite. Ha ha ha!'

'Are you sure this is the man, sir?' muttered Gaffer strongly.

'Yes. Look at the hat.'

'That doesn't mean anything, anyone can—' And he took out an identical hat, shoving it on.

'Take it off!' hissed the Mayor. 'You'll upset the bastards and they'll open out, wrapping us tightly in the tissues *they* consider least important to the smooth running of their beautiful body.'

'I *beg* your pardon?'

'Enter, children,' called the Conglomerate in exaggerated euphoria. 'I'm a surgeon who loves his work.'

'Did you hear *that*?' Gaffer whispered, but was pushed aside by the Mayor.

'Gentlemen,' the Mayor hailed as he strode in – he halted as the steaming environment hit his visor. Behind him, Gaffer entered the carrion stench of the conference room with a look of awe. The fungal walls moved with pumping lungs and the trickle of blood like shower runoff. Tall harps of tendons leaned together, taut with a webbing of catgut and hamstring. The Conglomerate itself was a pulsatile labyrinth of muscle, gelatinous pockets and hanging ganglion. A scorpion chandelier swarmed near the ceiling. The floor flowed and ratcheted with lobster growth, so much that it had bonded into one living mass. Amid venting steam and occasional pattering leaks of fluid, the Mayor stepped over slugs of slippery gut and approached the Conglomerate. 'You're looking well.'

'We bask in illness, idly invoicing the masses,' trilled a voice through a scalloped layering of fat. The hat fell to the floor, splashing in a dark puddle. 'We're so powerful it's not even funny. I sent for you to hear some entertaining evasions. How goes the campaign.'

The Mayor took another small step forward, holding aside a cerebral bag suspended from a snarl of veins and giving them a smile. 'Oh, we're three-deep in lobsters round there. M'lawyer here suggests we sell them as food for the poor. Other than that, everything's hunky dory.'

'I cannot agree with you,' came a voice from another part of the blubber mound. Rising steam faded and revealed sweaty detail. 'There is the matter of Cyril. He seems to have escaped your control. A manifesto has appeared, debasing your initial pitch. We have reports of people doing poncey dances against the crowd control barriers.'

Rudloe was rattled. 'It's the posters, gentlemen. Cyril it says, but nothing to do with my concept of the bastard. Staring thing with antennae. He purportedly invented concern.'

'Demon deals have been a feature of your campaign in the past, Rudloe – their dangerous wingtips brush you like a menu card. You're sure he's not one of yours?'

'I made up the Cyril cult so I could get those mugs into the shed and extort more levy for you, as you demanded, asked – but now a real Cyril cult is saying it may even disband so people won't have to contribute, you see? They've taken it out of my lily-white hands. Despite my calling dibs on the idea.'

'Dibs? There's no dibs in politics.'

'A swindler cannot afford to be headstrong,' another

mouth pitched in. It was situated between two black bellowing lungsacks. 'Best to be a team player, like us.'

'See the scope and grandeur of our biology. How much blood it takes to run. Hungry means angry. The red levy is all we ask of you, Rudloe. And your office depends upon our sanction.'

'What should I do?' said the Mayor. His voice was brittle, about to break. 'Put my own misshapen head in the noose? I'm the poor bastard who has to stand on that bony balcony flinging bacon and blennies to a rabble of rogues and madmen aren't I? Well?'

'Shut down the blood clock – tell them it's rusted and needs lubricating with some more of the rich stuff. Jam it just before twelve, that'll get them panting. Convince them they prosper through witnessing prosperity.'

'You underestimate the Cyril charlatans,' the Mayor ventured. 'Mournful speculation is circumvented by the strong drink of disobedience.'

'We never forbid or rebuke – leave that to the young generation. We present a choice. Find the hijacker who composed that childish tract. Alternatively.' A red arm extruded from the mass and indicated a ribbed exhibit revolving slow in the gloom, picked to a mere dangle of bones and gristle. 'You will no longer appear in your mirror.'

Watching the Mayor quake, Gaffer was dead impressed. Advancement perched pecking on his shoulder.

Skittermite manipulated a piece of clay into a semblance of Barny's face, plugged it on to his beak, and ran Gregor down with a tricycle. The scene was ignored by the majority of passers-by, who were used to Gregor failing at the top of his lungs. But a huddle of initiate fuseheads, who had been on the verge of approaching the holy one for wisdom, witnessed the blasphemous act and swore vengeance against the retreating Barny. Perhaps his punishment would form the centrepiece for a foam party. Gregor, meanwhile, they left thrashing in the dust. Holiness was long term, sin required immediate attention.

Barny entered Snorters Café to meet Magenta Blaze and found Edgy flailing under the weight of a frown. 'Bubba – just the man,' Edgy said, forcing him to sit down. 'You've gotta help get Amy's stupid poetry published – your name was on that dog book, officially you're the author.'

'Am I?'

'Yes. Why d'you think they had a cardboard cutout of you in the bookstore?'

'For being a loyal customer.'

'You sick sonofabitch, there's no way I can do this alone.' Edgy quoted a poem called 'Stood Up By Plantin Edge':

> *black dreaming*
> *telegram café*
> *arrive nine years late*

'I wish I could help you, Edgy, but even if I worked at the publishers I wouldn't take that bollocks.'

'What do you prefer – *We Are Taunted on Two Levels* or *Taunt Us on The Double*?'

'I prefer death.'

'Oh I guess you're right. How's the snake?'

'Tired and under pressure.'

'Why? Nothing's expected of her.'

'Oh right – only coiling, rearing up, rippling, and lying still as though dead while people speculate within earshot and call the authorities. How long before you'd crack under the strain?'

Edgy gave a noncommittal grunt.

'Then there's the Deadly Snake Contest to worry about. Balaclava Lewis and his bloody mamba are the favourites. Maybe I'm pushing Misses Kennedy too hard.'

'I don't know, Bubba. You here to break it off with the Blaze?'

'I'm going straight for the bust.'

'Better do that before you break up with her.'

Barny nodded. 'So what about this wolf tart you recommended?'

'Oh yeah, you'll see – it dilates the entire front of your face. Waitress!'

They ate some wolf tart and took turns dilating their face, bursting blood vessels in the nostril and forehead area. It's a man thing. Finally Magenta Blaze entered all smiles and ended their simple joy.

'Hello, darling, just . . . puffing our cheeks out a bit.'

'Wish I could stay, Madge,' Edgy called, standing. 'But there's something terrible Barny needs to lay on you. Pretty soon you'll be sobbing the place out like a lost child. See you, Bubba.' He skanked out.

'This all sounds very intriguing,' said Magenta, shunting into the booth. 'What's all these posters saying CYRIL WON'T BLOW HIS NOSE?'

'I don't know, I'm not political,' said Barny, his face still pullulating a little from the tart. 'This is what I'm saying, I'm not interested in politics, I'm not a trouble-maker, I'm not a high flyer, I'm not loud, I'm not into spreading it around.' Barny wound up for the Power Shout. Seven cannon followers burst in and began dragging him from the booth. '*I'M NOT WHO YOU THINK I AM!*'

'Yeah, right,' they snorted, wrestling him out of the café and into a plain van.

Five minutes later Barny stood before Rod Jayrod in the Powderhouse, surrounded by votive violence. Jayrod leaned forward, resting one wrist on a huge gold monstrance. 'Well, don't that just beat the biscuit. Barny "Nature Boy" Juno. You profane this temple.'

'I was dragged here.'

'Yes, but I see no reason to refrain from such a belter of a phrase. You profane it anyway. First you bury a lizard and drop your trousers during the eulogy, then you set an alligator upon one of our assassins, and today you run down one of our members, a certain Gregor, on a tricycle. Then you set upon him. According to eye-witnesses the number of punches to his belly ran well into three figures. You deny it, I suppose.'

'Yes, ma'am.'

'I'm afraid I find that difficult to believe. Don't you, guys and gals? Juno, you are some piece of work. It's common knowledge you consider yourself too, quote, swell, unquote to bother with doctrine. We know all about your trouble with demons.' Jayrod kicked back, lazy and powerful. 'Sweeney. A white trash devil.'

'Oh yeah,' muttered Barny – he had forgotten.

'I cannot understand why people object to our practices,' Jayrod declared. But when Barny began explaining it to him, Jayrod turned blandly away. Catching on, Barny's captors took another try at his face, buried their beliefs there – Barny was on the floor.

'And in addition to all this, you are one of the founders of the Cyril movement, the manifesto of which states' – and Jayrod referred to a leaflet – ' "Dash across the graveyard with a surfboard." A dubious sentiment at best. And where's the mention of our glorious cannons? The contrail left by a velocitous corpse as it breaks the sound barrier? Only one man had the skill to guide the fragments of the status quo – Wesley Kern. He built a portable cannon, handheld, by some means. Our altar once held it . . .'

Thinking about the Wesley Kern gun which resided at the Juice Museum, Barny became anxious. He had a habit of eating small, struggling trolls when under stress, and he pulled one of these from his pocket now – dozens of Cyril leaflets exploded out with it.

'Cyril lies!' shouted Jayrod, pointing like a dart. 'Right spang in the middle of the church! And what's with the troll?'

'I know a story about Kern,' blurted Barny, trying to remember what Chloe had said. 'One afternoon Kern decided he wanted to put the world to sleep, so he beat the hell out of everyone. And he killed the Mayor and stuffed a pineapple in his mouth, and photographed it. And he bought fifty pineapples and fed them to a load of kids, then sold seventeen more to the Mayor. And he campaigned for funds in the bathroom, saying, "The past has contained freedom – don't think of escape." And the doves began developing earlobes, so Kern kept one in a bell jar and killed it, and this dove became a shaman who manufactured bead curtains for a living. And Kern hoped that in the future his crazy antics would be celebrated every afternoon with a huge fiesta, culminating in an auction of collector's cards depicting . . . vapour.' Barny's face flummered with a wolf tart aftershock.

All activity had ceased in the temple. Rod Jayrod was shaking his head in reproach, while others regarded Barny with baffled disgust. Barny bit into the pudgy troll.

Jayrod gathered his wits. 'Yes. Well, you'll all be glad to know this diecast outrage won't go unpunished. Delicate fruit demands the hammer. It is almost the hour – prepare the Pit of Inconvenience.'

Barny was bounding across the altar in a jiffy, springing at the lip of the Powdermouth. Rod Jayrod became more bent out of shape than ever. 'Transgressor! Is everyone seeing this?'

Fuseheads were climbing the blast walls in antic frenzy, stilt babies striding near the iron face but not daring to make contact.

In the mouth of their pepperbox god, Barny was scrabbling around in a ratcheting trash of floor lobsters. It seemed the Powdermouth really did purify the church on the hour. And when that hour arrived, they atomised – Barny blurred across the temple, shattering the stilts from beneath a baby and blasting through the grand front doors.

Magenta Blaze strode across the main square, where the town hygiene department were spraying the 'speaking truncheon' with foam cement. Magenta made a neutral sound.

Barny was such a crazy guy. All that stuff about – what was it – not political, not loud, not a high flyer, not into spreading it around?

She stopped abruptly, thinking: or maybe he really was trying to break something to her.

Before she could pursue the notion she saw Barny flying through the sky, bellowing like a bastard and dispersing in his wake a litter of printed sedition.

7

Mad Cyril

Don't eat corks – there are waiters for that

The Mayor watched as a group of workmen laid into the speaking truncheon with chainsaws. The cement cladding had failed to set and it was a messy business. When a swarm of killer bees erupted from the saw wounds, the Mayor quickly slammed the balcony window and wheeled at Max Gaffer in a foul and vengeful mood. 'Cyril smiles a block away and obsessional fringe groups are born. Where's Turbot with the new speech?'

'Disappeared, sir.'

'Probably standing in the high street doing quickdraw with his willy, that's all we need. The Conglomerate'll drink paraffin through my bloody spine. Have you stopped the clock?'

'Yes, sir. That writhing anatomical stew you call a committee, I'm curious, are they human?'

'Of course, how else could their joint intelligence and morality be less than their individual intelligence and morality?' The Mayor started hauling on his containment suit, switching his cigar from hand to mouth to hand. 'I've been thinking, Max, how about calling this place Rudloe Manor? I mean, that's the style, isn't it? Slot-eyed armour on the landing, etc. And no one else will ever preside here.'

'Outstanding, sir.'

'Have you sorted the lobsters?'

'Yes, sir. The poorhouse owners realised if they take on our bugs they'll generate an almost equal number of their own – it's a helluva deal.'

'Good. Put a skirt on, Max – we're going to a Cyril meeting.'

Caged with worry, Gregor barely registered the worshippers doing sacred cannonball dives into the pool. He stood before Rod Jayrod in bad shape, his arm broken, his head reeling with crammed dogma. 'Fusemaster. I have brought this deformed wren as tribute.'

Jayrod blew out his cheeks. 'Well. As you're aware, I can't accept, or even take seriously, your bid for velocity without a full recital of the Ballistic Catechism. I can make no exceptions, not even for one to whom the Powdermouth has spoken.'

'Really?'

'The weak wipe their nostrils on the passing windshield.'

'The weak?' Gregor considered that by this estimation he must be as feeble as a strand of cress.

'It's just routine, I'm sure you'll do fine. Put the wren over there and assume the position.'

Gregor sat in a comfortable armchair.

'Why is traffic louder than roses?'

'To rise above beauty.'

'In which grabbing of one's own body is the stance of hero assumed?'

'No grabbing of one's own body.'

'What manner of years has it been since we made any sense?'

'Donkey's.'

'By what does the good man escape this world?'

'The seat of his pants.'

'Why do we ignore our ears?'

'Ears are not important.'

'Wet the face of a cow and what do you get?'

'A cow with a wet face.'

'What's the preferred entrance to a cake tasting?'

'Rising from a pit of smoke.'

'How shall we react to those who deplore us?'

'Move along deploring.'

'What sort of certainty can't choose?'

'A certainty in being wrong.'

'Why have you left your post?'

'Diligence bores me.'

'Why avoid capture?'

'Hostaging has no repartee.'

'Why look always forward?'

'Otherwise to discover would be to admit we didn't know.'

'Who is frisky and reasonable at the same time?'

'No one.'

'How are you spelling that?'

'Bite me.'

'How is space a comfort?'

'My face is only local.'

'Bulk lard at a monthly premium?'

'Crawl through tobacco straw to sign.'

'Forget to release the cagedancers long enough and?'

'Bugs take over the entertainment.'

'What is the lordly function?'

'Sitting in our roots, lords make illness of energy.'

'How can you believe you're normal?'

'In a matter of hours.'

'What is the advantage in dissolution?'

'The same advance in sensation will crumble my pursuers.'

'Why human?'

'Because we needed contours.'

'Why keep it modern?'

'Classic drama requires the description of various specialities.'

'What's buck-passing?'

'A suitable use of my time.'

'Why do you snigger?'

'Respect saddens me.'

'Of what do we say, "It's just procedure"?'

'Our flayed rejoicing.'

'Life holds out for stature and what does it get?'

'A belly.'

'Why confess?'

'Truth allows my demeanour to relax a couple o' seconds.'

'Monuments?'

'Hold memory in place, away from hearth and home.'

'Popular pints are never?'

'Green.'

'How far below the table can a dog go before he's performing a miracle?'

'Unknown.'

'How may persuasion be increased?'

'Suggest it in a lovely garden.'

'If imagination was ample I'd have twenty perfect legs – you?'

'A hen.'

'What freezes blood?'

'Window witches.'

'Tacky happiness?'

'White earphones.'

'How can we save money on personnel?'

'Pay the vision of them but not the people.'

'A badger will never don gloves but may remove them – why?'

'Badgers do not like wearing gloves.'

'Final goal?'

'No re-entry.'

'When a man blurs, does he cease to exist?'

'Yes.'

'Blasphemy!' Jayrod screamed, his face rigid with fury. 'You've misunderstood everything! And you consider yourself worthy to wear the blue touchpaper in your lapel? Goodbye without delay!'

Amid consternation and stares of grim disappointment, Gregor was ejected legs-first from the Powderhouse.

The meeting shed was in back of a derelict yard growing nothing but ovens. On the way they'd been harassed by a loogy-eyed bastard trying to sell lucky heather and brandishing a baby. 'What a darling little child,' Max Gaffer cooed. 'And that will be your undoing.' They had walked on, the Mayor glad both of his disguise and his containment suit. To conceal the visor he had wrapped his entire head in a golden turban. As well as a floral print dress, Gaffer had also seen fit to wear a set of antlers.

'Never fear, Max,' the Mayor whispered as they neared the entrance. 'Such meetings attract a certain kind of fanatical coward. A grab bag of god-gobs and debt-dancers. Lantern slides and dolly music. A paid-entry platitude meeting. We'll be in a forest of bizarre beards.'

'We find it advisable to keep our beards transparent around here,' remarked an unsmiling man at the door. 'And there's no charge.'

'Ah, all to the good,' blustered the Mayor. 'I'm impatient with restraint.'

Mohair pants filled the chapel. It was all wooden

benches and saucerlights – the new arrivals sat in the back row. Someone was shouting, 'Quiet – let Energy Maggot speak!' and on the makeshift stage a powdery old lady with a thin knife gave the scratchy cry: 'You all bug me. My furball husband was a thinker. He's been silky dust these twenty years. *That's* where you're headed.' And she picked up a toy wagon and tried to throw it into the audience, falling into the off. The Mayor saw that the backdrop consisted of a giant poster of the supposed Cyril.

An annoyingly zany hired host by the name of Rooster skipped beaming on to the stage. 'The expensive vocal stylings of Energy Maggot there.' Various resinous bubbles from his nose wrought unqualified dismay among the onlookers. 'And for those of you who've just joined us, welcome to today's Cyril cult meeting, sponsored by Stampede Products, "The firm that flirts with danger". Sit in these corners and be late for your responsibilities. Remember, society is a useless display and your head splits with duplicated material. I've just been handed a memo. It says there's a copper firefly in the sandy hand of the manager. And a note from F.D.A. Bonfire offering apologies for his absence. "I am so changed I fear you would not know your old friend." Ha ha ha – what a guy. If you want to flap your distorted jaw about anything, come on up – but first, here's Prancer Diego, who is not particularly brilliant in any way.'

Prancer took the stage in parrot-bright colours, setting up several high-ticket driftwood sculptures of his arse. 'Fascism is born of the idea that progress can reach a conclusion. Into a tirade you must schedule one snorting sound and three flubbers of the gob. No waste and no relaxation of stance. If relaxation occurs, re-establish continuity with a single step forward. Bake no pies during the address. Insist on nothing, but know in your heart that your people are long-horned and random, wild in their thoughts and utterly loyal to you, gorgeous.' Then he flew off the handle, yelling in a bogus dialect. He leapt from the stage and began striding down the aisle like a god. 'This carnage is doing my nut in,' he trumpeted. There followed an ugly clash of faces. Trying out the intended motion of an accuser, Prancer committed welcome and all was resolved. By this time Doctor Perfect, his brain sweating like damp clay, was on the stage bemoaning the lack of initiative re the north canyon. The foreshortened flyover was dotted with exploding sloths and anyone trying to vault the canyon by this means was blown apart, further shortening the road stump.

'On the plus side, yes, there's melons for all. Against it there's the matter of noses. Our nostrils are inescapable and will doom us all, believe me I know. And if Cyril invented concern like they say, shouldn't he begin constructing a bridge at once?' But everyone was bored with this subject and began shouting him down, pausing only briefly when he claimed, 'My skeleton is, however improbably, that of a zebra,' in a crass bid for popularity.

'We need an aeration parish to buffer the evil,' someone shouted, and was ignored as doomed Eddie Gallo stepped up.

'Why are we carrying on like this when the hot twilight air is full of flies? Why not lean on the pasture bars and watch it all? Bumble bees the size of dogs. These are our treacle days. And it's all nice and legal.' Gallo then embarked upon a discussion of tea biscuits so involved that even his close friends could make neither head nor tail of it. The last thing they let him say was something like 'there are many times the one shape and then my biscuits go away'.

During a bit of commotion the Mayor's bored scrutiny

fixed on the light above him. He squinted toward it, half-standing. Within the delicate bulb, where the filament should have been, was strung a sentence: 'I am trapped here and will die.' The Mayor sat down again. Maybe politics wasn't so random after all.

'Reliable old doomed Eddie Gallo,' chuffed a citizen sitting next to the Mayor. 'Congenial, covered in dove run-off – he's one o' the good ones.'

Unfailingly obliging, doomed Eddie Gallo gave way to a man wearing a corrective shirt, who did a victorious turkey trot across the stage before even saying anything. Then it became evident that the man had no intention of saying anything, and he was wrestled awkwardly from the limelight. Kung Fu Snorter claimed the right to read a lecture on the subject of 'My Eighth Belly'. But after two hours it dawned upon the assembly that he intended to prelude the talk with a thorough treatise on the first seven, and he was punched to the floor by a dozen citizens before he had reached the second. Another man announced, 'You'll love my skull,' and began tearing the skin from his face, at which alarmed onlookers sprang up and restrained him. The lights guttered, crackled and stayed on, causing only a fall of dust.

Later the patch-eyed E. H. Hunt dragged a heavy treasure chest on to the stage. His mane of white hair glowed under the stage lights. 'Beyond these shores I've met people all the colours of a fusewire. A half-decent star can take you anywhere. There's balloon fish out there that enjoy nothing so much as kissing a man. Hundreds of 'em. Think about that. No difference between drinking and puckering if you're a fish. Porpoises take care of themselves . . .'

There were groans of disinterest from the audience – these mythical so-called 'fish' and other 'ocean wonders' were Hunt's obsession. He told long, elaborate stories which could have been believed were it not for his insistence that they occurred on or even in salt water. Moonlight in the ship lanes, cults plunging a hunk of godstatue into the ocean, the burdenhead lying in sways of wrack. Hunt was growing belligerent. 'The iron shark circled, parrying our oars. Satisfied? Yes, my red chest seam goes wherever I go. Land leaders? Appeasement's a narrow reef – just forget 'em.'

Mayor Rudloe suddenly realised that Hunt had a beard like a shovel. He turned to Max Gaffer, whispering in outrage, 'That one's beard isn't transparent!'

The whisper was amplified by the audience's desperate need for distraction and all eyes fixed upon him. 'Maybe turban boy would like to share his thoughts with the rest of us?' asked Rooster, standing from the front row.

'That's right,' blurted the Mayor, bolting to his feet, 'you think I don't understand, you buoyant bastard? And why hasn't the Mayor been mentioned even once?'

'Because he's a depraved moron who sleeps in a fungus trench,' muttered someone in the crowd, to general agreement.

'Yes,' added another, 'and ugly, very.'

'Chubby too. Anyone that chubby wants watching.'

'All right,' yelled the Mayor, 'apart from being depraved, ugly and chubby, what's the problem?'

'Well, the Gubba men for instance – what are they?'

'On standby,' claimed the Mayor stoutly. A demon had long ago tattooed a magic phrase on to his left forearm, but this was hidden by his containment suit and thick disguise.

'Why are you defending him?' asked Prancer Diego. And he stalked forward, his avian head crooking this way and that in scrutiny. 'A box suit?'

'I've seen enough,' barked the Mayor urgently, tugging at Max Gaffer's arm. 'We're leaving.'

'Oho! It's like that, is it?' And as the two strangers scuttled up the aisle amid jeers, Prancer yelled after them. 'So regret me! Leave it to the real men, mister! Seeing duty's shape and the lake of deeper wealth I did a backward flip into the latter!' He slowed up, chuckling to himself. 'Technicians of the flaming man evaluated me as purposeless – quite likely my information was indeed out of their way. Everything's locking in, boys!' After the pair had left he shot his cuffs and started swanking around, strutting like a bastard so that everyone instantly wished him dead.

Unseen by the assembly, the demon Dietrich hung from a ceiling beam. His mutagenic disguise had failed and inner bone serrations were even now trying to elevate his expression, tearing through the skin in an explosive slake and locking into place as slimy, impractical tusks.

Blinded to the upper world, Sweeney had sent Dietrich above to assess Skitter's progress. Dietrich had never had great confidence in the little dingbat, but judging by these bizarre proceedings, the imp was frenzied with his own agenda. In pride of place at the head of the meeting hall hung a massive, bleached-out portrait of Skittermite himself.

8

Yer Wrath

Magic can puddle in the john

In a steel chamber at the rear of the chef school, Master Chef Quandia Lucent praised a drifting, finned backbone suspended in a painted cabinet. A group of students knelt in supplication.

'Human rights run counter to table manners,' the gilly fiend was sibilating eerily. 'This is our advantage. Necrotic flesh, insect paste and slatternly service.'

'They'll take it,' said the Master Chef, head bowed. 'They'll take it and smile.'

'Your ruthlessness does you credit,' queezed the creature. 'Each man will embrace his flaming portion. Leave me now.'

Quandia fastened the doors, closed his frown and the cabinet moment ended. 'We have a problem,' he told the assembled chefs without preamble. 'The Cyril meetings. I attended one disguised as a sane man and E. H. Hunt was there, talking about salty fish. What if he convinces them that those creatures really do exist in free abundance in the baffling ocean? Lets slip that they're edible? How long do you think everyone will keep swallowing pasta? And something else. The poorhouse have drastically reduced their pasta order – say they're going to dish out "mystery broth". That place is plastered with Cyril posters. We cannot allow such changes in the status quo. Recite the creed.'

The crew gave a mighty cry: 'Garbage, at crippling prices!'

Half drowner, half current, Noam B. Turbot picked among crustacean rubble and hopped dismissively over tidepools full of flimsy critters and general lassitude. He was no fan of the seafront with its outsidey wind and long situation but somewhere along here, he was sure, was an entrance to the Juice Museum – there he'd find some life. Fertility, nourishment; even rare volumes for the plundering. He'd surely earned that right. His self-denial just went over people's heads.

Too late he saw the Announcement Horse. This declaiming steed was worse than useless. Brandishing civilisation by way of excuse, he trafficked his knack for formal anguish and the stained iron body grew yearly heavier with brooding. He stood where beach tar and brown seaweed thin as audiotape darkened the rocks. A sepulchral chime rang out as Turbot tried to pass unnoticed. 'Turbot. You'll hear the devil's granulous footfall on the driveway.'

'I beg your pardon?'

'Death stares at our wrath like a babe at an equation. Slow into chains, nothingness is granted. We try to live by the false boon of law's detail. Yet only nature's detail is infinite.'

Turbot looked down – on the sandbed stupefactoids of every shape glittered together. Clinking rustacles were moving with the tide.

'Long ago from the sea things like armoured ears were caught and eaten. The ocean floated with sieve glands and living samosas. Today, what with the waves coming constant toward me in all their variation, it creates the illusion of progress, merely. You should try it.'

'Why should I?' Turbot demanded.

'You hope to slit open information and stuff your scalp. But the rain of cracked ownership works through the false door.'

Turbot was short of breath. He darted an orange cloth about his face and threw it over a passing butterfly. 'You presume too much. I mean, what are you? Eh? So there. I mean, situate me in time by the unique heart I hate in.'

'We are all sunk with tenure,' the Announcement Horse boomed, unmoving. 'Revelation too late. Keys past, useless but for a stranger's door.'

'Speak for yourself,' spat the speechwriter, and repeated it at a petulant yell. He stalked away down the beach.

The barnacled sentinel remained staring out to sea, water slocking up in the rocks.

Part of a Pennyground field had been cordoned off for the Deadly Snake Contest and a few spectators stood by unsure whether to be hearty or hesitant. Tony Fleet stepped into the contest area with Rubber Hose. 'This snake has a bill. No, only kidding.'

'What's interesting about that?' asked Barny, peering into the basket where Misses Kennedy was coiled.

'Just a joke to jolly us all along, despite the extremity.'

'We're here by choice, Tony, it's not terrible.'

'I suppose you're right. I still feel the need to joke about old Rubber Hose here though – don't I, Rubber? Don't I?' And he shook his face point-blank at the snake. 'I love ya! I love ya! Yes I do!'

'Calm down, Tony,' said Balaclava Lewis, affronted at the display.

'Look at the mug on him,' Tony continued.

'Destroying us is his idea of making a start,' Lewis told Barny.

'No one's destroying anyone,' Barny stated. 'Why don't we all just calm down. Is Sid ready?'

Golden Sid was strapped into an airlock throne, as pale as a shipwreck skeleton. His glasses magnified haunted eyes. The twisted fibre of his body was dense with fear, immovable, barely leaking breath.

'Ready,' said Lewis, then smirked at Barny. 'Honour hour is coming.'

'Don't count on it,' chuckled Tony Fleet, and kissed Rubber Hose for luck.

'Am I late?' asked Mike Abblatia, dashing up with a slow-worm.

'Perhaps I object,' said Lewis.

'Well do you?' Barny asked.

'No.'

'Right then,' called Barny, 'Tony to start.'

It was traditional for each competitor to introduce his snake with a one-sentence oration. Tony Fleet stepped forward with his cobra. 'Conjuring unfailingly blood from my forearm with his fangs, Rubber Hose is a focus for my love.' And he draped the snake across the nose of Golden Sid. 'Acknowledge the screaming, Balaclava Lewis,' Tony said as Sid reacted with loud cries.

'They're good enough,' Lewis conceded without real enthusiasm.

'You'll never tame the loops outta my baby,' smiled Tony, looking on at Rubber Hose.

'He's a fine snake, Tony,' said Barny with a firm nod.

'Two minutes,' called Lewis and the snake was removed from the traumatised captor. Lewis lifted his mamba, Tamale Wired For Sound, from a polished heart pine box. 'With his tarragon scales and scorn for pomposity, Tamale Wired For Sound bails me out every time.'

Then he whispered, 'You are done waiting, fang brother,' and threw it at Sid. The snake landed on Sid's face with great apparent acrimony, and the timid man began releasing short coughs of pain with each shake of his body.

Lewis looked knowingly toward the others. 'I deposit the magnitude of this event now – winner I am.'

'Not so soon, Lewis – this is not Sid's last yelling opportunity.'

Presently, Barny produced Misses Kennedy from her basket and stepped forward. 'Having better manners than to shout from an adjoining room, Misses Kennedy enters filled with gossip and licks me with her thin tongue.' He dropped the viper from above, causing Sid to shriek like a girl and burst into wrenching sobs, all control lost, a pitiful sight.

'There's a note of calculated contortion in his acts,' sneered Lewis, sniffing.

'Sore loser,' sniggered Tony Fleet.

To humour young Mike Abblatia they let him step forward with his slow-worm, though by now Golden Sid was beyond perceiving anything. 'Slowworm Sadness understands me, and curls in silence round my right wrist.' And he propped the slow-worm on the frame of Sid's glasses.

'That's a class showing, Mike,' nodded Barny. 'You improve every year.'

'Really, Barny?'

Barny warded off the onlookers. 'Contest still in progress! Nerve-ending safety is not guaranteed!'

Gregor had been hauled so far off the track he could see his own profile in silhouette, way off to the west. He sure had a belly on him. Entering the bakery, he indicated a display cake and said he wanted it.

'The theme is an old one,' replied the proprietor, and coughed loudly. 'Apologies, señor. Sickness travels the land, making a cane of a red thermometer. Another cough and the division between us increases. Here is the cake. You're billed in the side picture over there – a painted version of you dwells in the landscape.'

'You mean all fiscal matters are processed in that acrylic world.'

'I dare you to deny it.'

'I don't.'

'You are wise, señor.'

Now Gregor stormed into the shaman's yard and complained of shoddy brainwashing. Whole days had been hijacked by a stranger's agenda, all for nothing apparently. 'Edgy swears by you and your dumb tricks – maybe you can get me to see this stupid god who started it all. He's down in the creepchannel supposedly and I don't know how to navigate.'

'I'll try. Sit on the rock-feature there. What's that?'

'Some sort of cake.' Gregor dropped down near to Beltane, who was taking some slices of meat from a bag. 'So how did you get into this shaman nonsense?'

'Well I was walking along the riverbank and a brace of young otters started accusing me of every sin I could muster.'

'What sort of voice did they use?'

'Male, German accent, barking tone, as though recorded on an ancient wax drum.'

'And these were otters.'

'I know.'

'And after all this time you're still affected.'

'Well, I work all day, and . . . no, it never goes away. But I'm quite slim so it can't be all bad. Now, let's see what the arsenal cards have to say.' He drew a blackstrap and laid it down. 'Nephron. "Punch the apple from the branch." That's related to a myth, how mankind got the head involved.' He laid another down. 'Antihelix. "I badly need some respect." That speaks for itself. Loop of Henlé. "Did plans precede this disaster?" Great saphenous vein. "At least in detention the whirl of fists is private." Punctum—'

'Wait a minute!' Gregor yelled, standing. 'Is this all you're going to do? Is it too much to ask for anyone in this town to talk normally?'

'Barny asked the same thing. All right, Round One, I think I understand the problem anyway.' He dropped the cards into the pond and paced leisurely about the yard, regarding the tree-and-bird action. 'What mishaps we worship in extremity, eh. Your current position of tangling social disaster will one day grow uninteresting to you, Round One. Until then, what grief drains, flowers also drain.' He crouched at the pond, cupped water into his hands, and stood. 'This is called a cloachal star. What's the opposite of a trick?'

'That what-now?'

Beltane Carom flung the water toward Gregor and it blushed into a vortical membrane which swirled in mid-air as Gregor shrieked. Leaves and trash were being sucked into the twister.

The shaman yelled above the roar. 'Strange hole in the air, eh, that happens. There's a day between Thursday and Friday which the angels use. This yard is calibrated to it. Step through here and you're reborn in the corner of a redder room. Don't forget the cake.'

'Beltane,' shouted Gregor. 'If you were nothing more than an iron-willed moron, you'd tell me, wouldn't you?'

'Despair sits with truth in a blazing green garden.'

'What the fuck does that mean?'

'Never you mind – go, go, go, go!' He shoved Gregor

through the vortex, which sucked closed behind him. The shaman turned to the horizon. 'Fire in the hole!'

Gregor clenched his eyes against the storm of bloodwater which ended as suddenly as it began, then his sight cleared like the tide hissing back over shingle. Rendered numb with extremity, he was wandering through the weird obstetric subway known as the creepchannel, blasts of cold air blowing by him. Walls slimy as the innards of a mirror were dripping vitriol over heaps of pearl onions, fossilised eclairs and bent propellers. Gregor's sanity instantly sensed it was in a hardhat area. Once again his career as a boneless striver had left him entirely unprepared to face the day. His reserves of courage did not replenish automatically like those of others, and his quota had been low since he found a spider on the phone earlier. Sick with apprehension, he climbed slow up a technical ghost pocket into an endless migraine pattern of walk-in crypts and yellowed electrocution. He walked across a massive puzzle made of skin, realising afterward he should have gone around it like a traffic island. Sickstone walls dented with the grey alphabet began to change as he passed, curving into the smiles of lawyers. Then he tripped and slid quailing down a deeply sloping tunnel, accelerating through a daze of bone-flake confetti and almost dropping the cake. As he blurred along the cascade, darkness wheezing beneath him and elemental agony scorching his ears, he wondered how papers tackled this sort of thing in the lifestyle section. Maybe his reckless foray into damnation was frowned upon by the smart set – or flawed simply by his carrying this particular cake or screaming this particular way. There was so much to conform to, and to what possible gain? It was baffling to him.

He spent the next few hours edging thoughtfully along

some precarious meltstone ledges, eating his own mouth in fear, and remembering better times until finally he levered himself into a tunnel and lurched from a hole in the ground, his eyes like sun-dried tomatoes. He was in a vast ribbed cavern which banged with arcane industry and flashed with yellow air pain. There was a weird sense of imminence as Gregor, sick with apprehension, looked over at a movement. Lit by an opening in the smoke, there reared a colossal skeletal insect, its complex open-work body studded with ducts and scissoring mandibles. A coldwater heart was visible through epiurethane skin. The whole thing was enthroned in a veined, leathery halfshell.

Gregor took the liberty of flailing backwards as the creature regarded him with eyeballs of porous bone. But seeing as his luck was long ago cut off at the pants pocket, it barely mattered what he did now. Gregor stepped forward. 'Don't talk, okay? Just listen. Thank you for inviting me and my friends for jelly and ice cream. I didn't ignore the invitation, I tried to get here. If I'd known it was this easy to walk here I wouldn't have tried to drive over. And where's the parking? Did you consider that?' Gregor kicked at some red shapes on the floor. 'What are these little flesh brackets?'

'Gitterbants.'

'Gitterbants, that's what you call them, eh? You learn a new thing every day. So listen, I brought you a cake, here it is.'

'"Happy Birthday to Our Darling Little Boy". And what's that, a snow scene?'

'Yeah, a little fella skiing.'

The face of slowly maculate death armour shifted in the dark. 'Foolhardy, Mister One, but not the way you hoped. D'you really consider yourself as adept at that little game as your friend Juno? Protection through randomised innocence? Not you, and most certainly not here.' The demon ejected some gore from its ear nozzles. 'Oh, you run fast over turf but you're suited more for baiting Juno into—'

'Can I put the cake down? My arm's busted.'

'Don't interrupt while I'm detailing my infernal scheme – what's the matter with your arm?'

'That simple bastard Barny ran me over with a tricycle. I got a black eye too but that's going pale green now.'

'But he's your friend, yes?'

'Does he sound like one?'

'You mean he doesn't actually care what happens to you? I can't use you as bait?'

'Shall I put the cake on the sidetable of bones, then?'

'And a special occasion cake? Why bring it to me?'

Gregor smiled uncertainly. 'Isn't this a special occasion? I mean, here I am.'

'D'you take a special occasion cake wherever you are? And say "Here I am"? Get away from me!' And the demon kicked up with a mandible, exploding the cake.

'So we're quits, right?'

'Get out!'

Gregor jittered and ran.

When the blob-faced botch of a man had gone, Sweeney called down the Aspict. He watched as it extruded from the ceiling, but the worker demons were still attached, tinkering with its beautifully tooled acridity. 'It'll take at least a week, guv,' they shouted down. Sweeney sent it away again.

So the Round One was of no regard to Juno at all, and useless as bait! Sweeney knew enough about the world above to know that deliberate ramming with a stabilised bike was not an act of friendship.

Just then Skittermite darted in, scampering on the spot

and generally stinking up the place. 'Majesty yes thank you, I have turned the Round One against his friend by disguising myself as Juno and running him down with a tricycle.'

Sweeney darkened like a bottle filling with smoke. 'What? You bloody moron, I let him go because of your baffling actions! Are you deliberately wrecking my affairs?'

Skittermite was about to defend himself when the demon Dietrich entered with a large paper tube. 'I told you this skeletal tyke's brain was too close to his ankles. I visited a raucous meeting of the so-called Cyril cult above and here's a beautiful poster of their leader.' He unfurled the poster with a flourish – Skittermite's bleached features stared out above the slogan I AM CONCERN. 'Yes, he's making a power play of his own above as this Cyril fella. He must have been laying the ground for it the whole time everyone thought he was stuck in that drain.'

Sweeney turned his black ice skull toward the cowering imp. 'So you've been industrious. No sooner are you in their bandwidth than you install yourself as a gilly firebrand and influence the masses. What else were you planning – a demon flypast?'

'Your Majesty thank you, remember what Violaine said: "Power receives power." '

'*Violaine?* You dare . . .'

And Sweeney began pulling away from his chair, straining forward as pink stretches of gut flubbered and twanged like gum behind him, locking taut in mid-step. Skittermite sped chittering up the wall and between the ribs of the distant ceiling, vanishing amid crannies of infection. Sweeney turned to Dietrich with a yell that banged some enamel off his beak: 'Clip his wings!'

As Dietrich took flight into the rafters where a billion

hollow realtors dangled, Sweeney struggled against his extravagant anatomy, leaning away from the varicose muscle which bound him to the throne.

Behind him a white eye opened in the chairback. Slipping foolishly in the smashed cake, Sweeney was reeled in like a puppet.

9

Do Not Forsake Me Oh My Darling

Progress accelerates downhill

Fugitive from pursuer shadows rippling over walls, Skittermite hammered at the door of the Powderhouse. A face appeared in the doorcrack and sank away again. Voices.

'Monster outside.'

'Mouth dripping?'

'Dripping and it's a lulu.'

Pushing in and no illusions about his chances, Skittermite flew at the Fusemaster's shirt and hung there like a bat. He was still begging for sanctuary when the worshippers tore him away. A quick X-ray of his head raised more questions than it answered.

'A funeral crasher?' Jayrod barked. 'Explain yourself.'

Skittermite produced a ticket of gospel glass which he'd picked up here a few days ago and chirped the only piece of cannonical dogma he recalled. 'Without vice we are chill.'

'You petition for membership?' shouted Jayrod in hilarity, then stopped as though stung. He lifted a presentation fruitbowl under which lay a Cyril leaflet bearing the likeness of Skittermite. 'Sharpened face?

Telescopic eyes? Yay high? Cyril himself, here to tear my expensive shirt and yours!'

A rush of fuseheads lifted Skittermite aloft in a frisky way and shouted, 'Try my aerosol udder!' or something like that, hurling him into the frolic pool. He emerged with froth on his head and was told by everyone that he looked like a lamb. He almost digested himself with shame.

Edgy bumped into Magenta Blaze outside Snorters Café and in no time at all had her believing he and Barny were known as 'the Dull Boys'.

'And I can't pretend we don't deserve it,' he added. 'By the way, which do you prefer for a book of poems – *We Are Taunted on Two Levels* or *Taunt Us on the Double*?'

'*Flowers Are Lovely*,' she replied with a bright expression.

His smile frozen, Edgy backed away and continued toward Feeble Champ Books. The building perched on the edge of the canyon and it was easy to fling unwanted manuscripts from the window into this convenient abyss. In fact the office of Crash Test Nureyev projected over the drop, steadied by chunky wooden struts. Nureyev rose to greet Edgy as he entered. 'Plantin, glad you could come.'

'I reached the street according to the plan.'

'Good, good.' Nureyev seated himself behind a desk collision and the smog of cigarettes. 'Sit you down.'

Edgy indicated a hammered steel cardigan on the wall. 'What's that?'

'A reminder of the human cost. I lick it every afternoon.'

'Really?'

'Without fail.' Nureyev smiled wickedly. 'I've been looking again at Gort's manuscript. I admire your talent for finding these characters – Juno's dog book is a real hit. That chapter entitled "Dogs Are Blameless" is spot-on, no matter how much it grieves me. He's some kind of genius, though the couple of times I met him he denied it. In fact he acted like he didn't know what I was talking about.'

'Yeah, well, he's a card.'

'The second time I met him he was spreading some sort of ointment on a monkey's hand and kept telling me this was the quietest the chimp had ever been. What do you suppose that's about?'

'Er . . . I really came here to talk about Amy Gort, Mr Nureyev. As her personal agent I'm concerned about the presentation.'

'How so?'

'The title – she prefers *We Are Taunted on Two Levels* and I say *Taunt Us on the Double* – someone just suggested *Flowers Are Lovely* and I have to say I'm losing all perspective.'

'That's a mistake I wouldn't recommend. Nine mistakes I would recommend are: sneeze forty-eight feet of telephone wire across the sky; compliment a frazzled loser; triumphantly bring in a thing dangly-dead; hide an ambulance under your shirt; touch something glimpsed in tears; prepare a prison of ham, previously a sunlit limestone yard; take seventy-three years to get dressed; hook your scalp and pull; sign your memories over to me and stand silently outside my office.'

'It's a deal.'

'Plantin, these are all mistakes. You see you're taking it all too seriously.' He lit a cigarette and drew, regarding Edgy thoughtfully a while. 'You see the metal cardigan up there? It was given to me by an old-time writer by the name of Noam B. Turbot in his heyday. Man of letters.'

'Man of what?'

'Letters. Wrote *The Wedlock Trilogy*. Covered his marriage in *Against My Will*, his divorce in *Trying to Hide* and its aftermath in *Blessed Relief*. You see?'

'Dinner-party stuff.'

'Yes, middle-class tedium. I must have wished for his death a hundred times. Action was back and business blew random money into the flue. Bit him on one occasion. Fat off his arm tasted of coffee. We were running from an electrical storm once, hell of a thing – a stunning, crackling uproar. And he began to swerve for no reason I could see. I didn't mention it at the time. But then I had an unwise fit of temper. "I'm suspicious about you changing course suddenly when we were running from the electric storm the other night." Well he finally confessed but I had to physically pull the words from his face. Apparently he was running and decided maybe it wouldn't be such a bad idea to act like he knew what he was doing. And in the process he had some sort of vision concerning a giant kitchen full of bagels, sex and spare time. This, it turned out, was his plan for the future. Well, suddenly the day of success played out. He lost all humility and perspective. Boxes of pills were bashed aside by his face, he trembled, reeling across the hospital walls, beating off the menace of help and stammering like a bastard. Officials fumbled the rest. Now I hear he lives only to increase his past. Pity he ruined the storm with his apparent knowledge and adjustments. Meanwhile I remember my principles with a jolly nostalgia. And smoke cigarettes tasting of dead cat.'

'So Amy's poems, Mr Nureyev. You really do think they're good, right?'

'Plantin, I love this stuff. Give it to me and the lines are wolfed down like sausages. This one, "Certifying Puncher Horn":

'Nuns float on wheels
strangled my neck
mechanical daughters moving rapidly
fear transfigures

'Reindeer don't know that, do they?'

'No, Mr Nureyev.'

'Believe me, Plantin, hotels are pelvic, cowpats look like liquorice, a church organ sounds like cheese and a lion's a lion whichever way you slice it. Tears understand the page. Climactic fight in a grain tower and Bob's your uncle.'

'But, er . . . but the title, Mr Nureyev. What do you think?'

'I can tell I'm still not getting through to you, Plantin. Come here, I'd like to show you something.' He stood and led Edgy to a corner table cluttered with dusty office plants. In a pot on top of a thick ledger was a human head, a dead ringer for Nureyev's own but for its silver eyes. 'Isn't that something? Got it from Kenny Reactor at the hydroponic place, one of his little experiments. Completely vegetative, never moves, doesn't make a sound, nothing like that. I find it relaxing to water this guy and let it do my worrying for me. You know how I boost the soil? Wood pulp. Eh? Bookpaper. Eh? Isn't that beautiful?'

Edgy knelt close to the fungal face.

'Your man Juno's got the right idea, Plantin – don't measure yourself by all this. Life's elsewhere.'

The Feeble Champ building faced on to the rear of the mayoral palace and as Edgy emerged he saw Max Gaffer slinking around back there. The lawyer was supervising the loading of sacks into a van. This didn't seem significant until one of the sacks burst open over a workman and a jumble of bugs swallowed him alive.

*

Barny was dozing in a hammock, the house lopsided around him and loud with the green squeak of canaries. Grass grew out of the radio.

Edgy entered using the walls for balance. 'Bubba, wake up – I bumped into Magenta Blaze outside Snorters. I told her you're dull, we both are. I may have convinced her we're actually known as the Dull Boys.'

Barny looked blearily at Edgy. 'Dull Boys?'

'Yeah, I know the trouble you've been having.'

'You talked to her?'

'I think I set her straight on a few things. She says she loves it when you get assertive and start shouting.'

'She used those exact words?'

' "I love it when he gets assertive and starts shouting." '

'What was she doing when she said it?'

'Just looking at me and smiling.'

'In an amorous way?'

'Why would she be smiling at me in an amorous way as she said that?'

'Maybe she wanted you to shout at her, I don't know. I never know what's going on with her.'

'I don't know, maybe she meant something by it.'

Barny watched the chimps awhile. 'So what it boils down to is we don't know any more than we did before you spoke to her.'

'No we don't.'

'Well thanks, Edgy.'

Edgy sat on a gangplank, swinging his legs thoughtfully. 'You could tell her you had sex with the lion.'

'She'd just be impressed.'

'You didn't, did you?'

'Rest easy, Edgy. Look around. Slow lizards on the prowl. Cats scudding around the place. It doesn't get any better than this.'

'Yeah, you've got a nice setup here, Bubba.' They

listened to the hiss of the shade trees. 'Hey, that's what I wanted to tell you – listen to this.'

And Edgy told him about what he'd seen behind the mayoral palace. Walking past the poorhouse later, he had seen the same van unloading and a sign on the kitchen window in black Chinese ink: IN PLACE OF PASTA, IT WILL NOW BE THE POLICY OF THIS ESTABLISHMENT TO SERVE MYSTERY BROTH, A THICK SOUP WHICH IS WITH-OUT CHARM OR SURPRISE.

'You see what's going on there, Bubba?'

Barny's round, bland countenance showed that he didn't.

'Remember what old Bingo Violaine said? "Whispering is satisfactory only when it is overheard." Think about it, Bubba, the Mayor and his lawyer are feeding floor lobsters to the poor.'

Barny thought about it, blank. 'Animals need happy results.'

'So? That's what I'm telling you, isn't it? What are we going to do about it?'

Skittermite had returned to the Powdermouth, kneecap in hand. Marvelling at his sheer swagger at coming back, and jazzed at the idea of indoctrinating Cyril, they had given him their hopeless credo bound in a burnished volume. 'Learn the same thousand manners as these fellows,' Rod Jayrod had told him, spent with excess. 'It could be a setback or the opportunity of a lifetime. Either way, I'm okay.' And he dismissed him with a lax and peremptory twist of the hand.

Now the grease monkey sat in the poorhouse swaddled in a small blanket, spooning strange soup, absently unscrewing a scab and pondering the dogma. 'Showing your complaint to the sky, you'll be cold and out of range, footprints lost, smeared in the wind. Mince the clouds and drink the rain, fly, fly.'

He looked aside at a slack-jawed chump, who indicated a bug on the table. 'Hey – check out the standing caterpillar.'

Cramped with change, Skittermite returned to the writ. 'Watch a spear hit the horizon, re-create the first question.'

Blasphemy awareness? Arcana trumpcards? They wrote the same as they spoke. It didn't mean anything! This place and the everlasting happy sun, damn the sun! Where was the creepchannel's electrocutive bone cold? The vomit in the heart?

But a dozen grim breaths later, he quietly returned the information framed in despair.

Then all hell broke loose. Barny Juno and the scarecrow man erupted in upon giant wild animals, holding nothing back. 'Understand that you are always a lion, Mister Braintree,' called Barny Juno. The cat reared, pouncing bowls and cutlery from the tables. Sallow urchins ran screaming.

'This cat's so glossy it's almost frictionless,' yelled Edgy. The leopard gave a chewy snarl. 'Feel it.'

'I have, Edgy, and it is.'

The lion swiped a cook with a forepaw. 'You have purged suspense by knocking me out,' the cook claimed before falling.

'Deadly poison!' shouted Edgy, swiping a pan from an old man's hand.

The old man looked severe. 'To be struck in August: wrong.'

Skittermite was weeping tears like cough drops, order exploding all around him. 'The day you elected to ride into the canteen on a lion thank you,' he screamed, 'my strained trail faded for no one to follow.' Looking through the haze of flying soup and mind-boggling profanity, he saw that the men upon the fierce roarers were discussing the scene at hand as though it were over.

'In the confusion I stole this.' Edgy produced from his thin shirt a meaningless velvet colour swatch.

'Your mania for leopard-riding,' Barny smiled, 'has not destroyed you.'

Skitter's mind was dissolving like new bread.

10

Musclebound Freakout

Point enough and people will look at you

'Look at this,' spat the Mayor, slapping *The Blank Stare*. '"Frothing potion gets uniform thumbs-down because it's venom." And sightings of Cyril at the scene, shouting against the state. How can he be this organised? That meeting we went to was carved from raw spud.'

'Nothing to get hung about,' said Max Gaffer.

'With me pumping out evil at this rate? By the time we get back to the office it'll be rammed with lobsters again.'

They were sat in the back of the limo as it glided toward the Furfur district. Gaffer was slow and casual. 'Only a setback for your conscience, sir.'

'My hair was my conscience, I was glad when it went. We need a pain handle on the populace. A few drops of rain erase the benefit of thirst – what are we going to do? This Cyril's a popular guy – maybe we could welcome him into the mayoral race all patronising, say competition's good, new blood's welcome.'

'The less said about blood, sir. Defend the man in anagrams – play it safe.'

'You were born into an office, weren't you? Well let's

hope old speechbelcher Turbot's finally shambled home. A firm line's required. Straight from the shoulder, though naturally not mine. More stuff about the town clock as a symbol of something or other. Tricks and crafty betrayal, Max, that's the stuff, eh? At all costs they can't be allowed to know it's the same blood recirculating.'

'Agreed. They'll point to the gutted and say, er, something like, "Lookathem, eh? There's a bad thing."'

Gaffer was referring to citizens who had been overlevied and now lived as rattling freaks in the borderlands – people like Microlady and the Kite, shrunk and bloodless.

'The gutted? I look elsewhere for my terrors.'

'The Conglomerate.'

The Mayor tersely admitted that this was the case. 'Beef up security anyway. Thaw the Brigade and point them in the right direction.'

'Already done, sir.'

'You know, Max. Power's a funny thing. I was a toddler when I knew. They wanted me to walk, they insisted on it. The pressure was on, so my arms started moving. I spoke some loud words before I knew what I was doing. People said I had talent. At my urging the old settled routines became bravely superimposed with images of activity and change. That's what I am, Max. A force to be acknowledged.'

'My enthusiasm is inoperative, sir. There are people ahead of us.'

'Oh, a night's sleep'll forget 'em.'

'Outstanding, sir, but I mean the people are revolting.'

'The verb?' Rudloe jerked his attention to the window, clinging a hand to the glass and squinting out. The car had slowed into a crowd of citizens who were brandishing banner slogans such as TOO DRY ELUSORY DREAM and

MORTARED LORD — YES, YOU! and LET ROAD MURDERS YOYO and DESTROY YOUR MALE ROD and DELOUSE MY TARRY DOOR and TRY OUR LAYERED MOODS and MODERATELY SORRY DUO and YOU DRY ROADSTER MOLE! and ORATORS DYED YOUR ELM. 'What's this for? They're usually bone idle.'

The car was now stationary but for the shoving of the populace. The Mayor noticed that one man dressed in a mechanic's uniform was copulating with the fuel valve. Some of the crowd were carrying a huge inflatable bargain-hunter with bulging eyes, its fat arms floating aimlessly. Others kept pointing to their own nostrils, each individually and with a fierce and meaningful expression. The rhythm of this activity was both hypnotic and frightening. Two elected children bashfully pushed a set of giant wooden dentures into the face of the bargain-hunter. Bag-cheeked and billowing, it buckled and dented down until the bearers were dragging a flaccid tangle upon which the kids rode in delight, slime spurting from their gills.

'At least they're not saying "Destroy Mayor Rudloe",' said Gaffer.

Without the containment suit Rudloe had full access to the magic phrase tattooed on his arm — drawing up his sleeve, he took a gander: I HAVE MADE IT QUITE CLEAR THAT.

Clearing his throat, he slid open the roof hatch and stood to straighten his instincts out. 'I have made it quite clear that, er, our happy home Accomplice, an imploded enclave, is mandatory. This martyr's rodeo you call a protest — what do you think it'll achieve?'

The dot-eared GI Bill, nose as grubby as a graveyard dog, stumped pugnaciously up with a banner saying YORE A DOLDRUM OYSTER. Then he hauled the Mayor by the arm, toppling him into the mob.

The Mayor gripped his own throat, gasping pop-eyed. 'Manmade fibres!'

The Brigade were wandering nearby, looking at the trees. 'Lovely inspection, Sarge,' said the Deputy. 'We adore you like a mother.'

'Thank you, but one of you apes sighed like the air pushing out of a cushion – any guesses who that could have been?'

'T-T-T-T-T-T-T-Teddy?'

'There you go – was that so hard?'

'My abdomen,' said Teddy.

'What?'

'My abdomen bubbles . . . look, it's poisoned, pullulating – it looks like a brain!'

'What's the matter with you, boy? And here we are in the countryside and all?'

'He ate some soup at the poorhouse, Sarge,' said the Deputy. 'I don't know why.'

'Let's stop here and the main ones, that's me, the Deputy and Gibbs, will sit on that gate. You others, sit in a circle and look angry.' The Sarge sat on the gate and everyone followed his instructions. 'Lads, do you remember Karloff's Circus and the trouble it caused us? Never go to the circus, lads. Soldiers in the dim-lit sawdust ring talk through sewn lips, unheard – they're food for midgets and lions, their veins drawn out and dried to make the netting under the highwire. Their heads flattened and bolted to create the wheels which all fly off the mini car at once and bounce – there's a reason they bounce and that's the brains, being put to use for the first time.' Finished, he turned to his deputy, who brandished a dish.

'Snail, Sarge?'

'Don't mind if I do. What are they?'

'Snails, Sarge.'

'Snails. Don't mind if I do.'

'Get your face round that then.'

'What is it.'

'A snail, Sarge.'

'Snail. All right then. Eat it do I?'

'Eat it, Sarge, that's right.'

'What is it?'

'Snail – a snail, Sarge.'

'Snail.'

'A snail, Sarge. See? It's a snail.'

'Snail, is it. Well now.'

'Snail.'

'Snail, eh. Well, don't mind if I do.'

'Good on yuh.'

'Right.'

'You eatin' it then?'

'Eh?'

'You eatin' that?'

'What is it.'

Before the Deputy could reply, a cry rang out. The troops gazed toward a wide lane a way off, where the Mayor was being thrown into the sky by citizens galore. Max Gaffer too was being manhandled. 'Don't touch the underwear!' he was shrieking.

'That must have been the cry we just heard,' the Deputy muttered.

As they continued to watch, they saw the Mayor's driver being smothered in paste and relay monks dancing tauntingly before him with emeralds the size of boxing gloves. 'Merciful god!' screamed the driver. A roofmender wearing a dragonfly mask took a run-up and kicked a seabird into an unset loaf.

'Ah, Death, the incompetent visitor in red,' the Sarge commented.

As the Mayor stood restrained by pouting rioters, Prancer Diego stood point-blank in front of him, facing the other way. Then Prancer glanced at him negligently, seemed to notice him for the first time, and began jabbering about 'hook dames'. With a caw of laughter he suffered a whole-body convulsion which sent him sprawling. 'Stretch the chalk mark from this origin to the greyhound over there,' he began to say, but his words segued into another language as he waded down the road as though in a river, up to his waist. He thrashed deeper until finally the road closed over his vulpine head.

It had been a stressful day. Startled by a pop-up book, the Sarge had knifed the main character. Seeing his mistake and the resultant damage, he had cried for almost an hour. 'Shall I at least set my lads in order?' he asked himself now, and decided. 'Commandeer eighteen worms, boys.'

'What are we going to do, Sarge?' asked his deputy brightly.

'All kindness and concern,' said the Sarge, 'we'll go hog-wild for studying worms.' He stood down from the gate and fixed his face on the future. '*That's* what we're going to do.'

Reckless in his quest for plagiarism, Noam B. Turbot jettisoned the rotten plank he'd been using for buoyancy and waded to the grotto shelf. He had gambled that this low-roofed sea cave was an entrance to the Juice Museum and the bed and lamp on the inner shore suggested it was inhabited at least. Reaching the sandy ridge he looked back at the distant cave mouth. Albescent shapes played over the walls, teasing hundreds of drifty pleasures from his brain. A tunnel of damp limestone sloped upward into the rock. He followed it, fiending for head-food.

The tunnel walls became panelled with warmly po-lished wood, embedded with slide-drawer cabinets and foggy paintings. Turbot drew out a narrow drawer and found a weathered photo of Wesley Kern and Bingo Violaine larking about with what appeared to be an enraged grizzly bear. Another showed the bear asleep in a hammock. So far so good. Stuffing these into his pocket, he went on.

On an earth-floored landing, cupboards displayed code stones, a smoking rose, snake-tree gold, brittle scrolls and rusted shrike scissors. A framed picture was filling with seawater, historical victims looking out. Along the passage, Turbot stopped short as he was passing a little side-room. An old man, his face benign and wrinkled with smiling, sat looking into a teacup tattooed with vines and muttered to himself. 'Thirty days sipping tea has left me in charge of the moon's character, I defend it continually . . .'

Turbot ducked past, entering a room like the shell of a chambered nautilus and filled with the smell of burning sugar. Here was fusty junk and cherry gas, the essence of stuff pulsing through the air. He saw coloured glooms and rusting apples, tarmac heatwarp rising through blackberry bushes, heaven glimpses of the right thing done on some ethical afternoon. A wet garden of detail shifting with fresh sun. Emerald melodies chimed around him. He was as loose as the tired sky-muscles of the clouds.

He floated on into a chamber which smelt like rotten flowers, his heart buzzing hard like a beetle. A thousand cracked books lay amid arcane artefacts. A parchment portrayed the bowed ribs of fantastical lunar barges. Turbot opened a volume bound in rose leather. 'Gentle-men have many terms for the dead and many levels of decomposition. Their world is the final version, their actions already taken. They don't let go easily. Smiles are not a part of their worth. They grow ruins of judgement and class. Topics of interest may not awake them. Wounds spurt sand. Death for them is distinguished and garnished with dainty platitudes. Their frontier is delineated only by eyeliner. They say, "The true use of suspicion is a holy thing." They say, "Pursuit is a negotiation." They say, "Respect the paper." They are a beacon of absence.'

Turbot regretted having read it. Must explore, he thought, pleased with his adventure, the first in years. A fanned rack of stairs faded into the dark and he wandered down to a windy platform of architectural fragments and ancient statuary. There was a pediment with the slogan 'Love is the opposite of luck'. Must remember, he thought, and keep a hold of why I'm here.

Testing the environment beyond the platform, he found soft soil, and stepped tentatively on to this, walking into the cold shadows. On the way he passed something which looked like a folded, boulder-sized gallstone. A swerved human face was frozen in the mix, its palate reversed. There were structures ahead, and as he got among them he found that they were doors planted upright, frames and all.

All the doors had something attached to the back, something like a dry umbilical or withered tap root. Turbot went to the handled side of a door and pushed it open. He was looking into a starved hallway, bleak and trivial. A hollow wind cut through a universe of destitute oblivion, where the best hope was a depth of suffocation, deaf bones packed in soil. The sight crystallised in Turbot's mind as the purest mirror, showing him the dead wire of his reflection. Gnawed by a roaring vacuum he reeled back, toppling some monstrous ornament and collapsing against a step like the church kerb of a crypt. His frosted brain crackled audibly. Just his luck to get the empty mask.

11

Amoebas Are Very Small

Leverage is dulled on a soft man

Gettysburg, a demon of mystery skin and lightning-bug eyes, was sat in the shaman's yard chatting to Beltane Carom. 'You advise Barny Juno because you think he's a special case, maybe he is. But when Violaine prophesied the Beast Man and the downfall of my old master, the philosopher was sputtering through his own blood and brainwater. Maybe it isn't Juno. What's he got going for him?'

'Power through misdirection,' muttered Carom. 'Yeah, not much.'

'So what's with this?' The defector demon produced a copy of *The Blank Stare* with the headline CYRIL'S CONCERN ESCALATES. 'How's this helping Barny? If he's implicated who'll protect him? And what are you doing to shield him from Sweeney?'

'You still don't understand this place, Getty.'

Gettysburg stood, a white giant with a spike-mine head. 'Maybe I don't, but I consciously chose this set of dimensions – I sometimes think you people take them for granted.'

As Getty re-emerged into the alleyway he glimpsed

jerky motions in a corner – a little sprite with a head like an anode capered up all desperation.

'Is that little Kermit? Last time I saw you you were working on that subspace extension.'

'Mr Getty,' Skittermite rasped. 'Impossible. How to be here, the Powdermouth, chaos, I can't—'

A shadow stiffened into form and began walking. 'Boy, the detail of decorum is disgusting.' Dietrich strode into the light. 'Why consort with his type – the shaman? Inconveniencing everyone with signs and wonders. He picks out of happiness an answer that would die else-where. The assumption that if you got a good philosophy it'll stand up under fire from the likes of us. Accomplice suits a vanilla demon.'

Gettysburg smiled. 'You're so transparently relieved to be able to talk about it all, Dieter. Why keep coming back? I think you fantasise of being stopped.'

'No. Autonomy is one tooth, useless.'

'You're wrong, it's owning your own jaws. Look, let's just try and have a nice time, shall we?'

Skittermite looked on as the two giants faced off. Dietrich turned to him. 'Send a weak link after a weak link, how dumb was that? Time to take him in.'

'Run, Kermit, run!' shouted the white demon, slamming a claw around Dietrich's throat. He hissed into his face. 'Heroes yearn for mistakes. It's natural.'

'Call yourself a hero?'

'I meant you.'

He hurled the paravamp backward. Dietrich stumbled, steadied himself. Skittermite was gone.

'So the sun's come out like that, eh?' Dietrich breathed.

Gettysburg blinked his milk-opal eyes.

'Mascot,' spat the paravamp, and deployed his wings.

Gettysburg was left staring at the minus smear of his departure. 'That is one conflicted demon.'

Mayor Rudloe and the lawyer dragged into the office and collapsed into chairs, standing again to repeat the relief of the experience. 'What the hell was that about? Emeralds, lard? Did you see that abnormally bearded failure with the net? The satanic runners? And your hired goons were just skylarking, off to the right.'

'Studying worms.' Max Gaffer plucked a dead fern from his torn trouser leg. 'Yes. Yes, I accept that they could have helped more.'

'God almighty. If this trend persists we'll be seeing our own bones. Make some tea, will you.'

'Naturally I refuse.'

Rudloe sagged back in his chair, hopes draining out with his exhalation. He glanced aside at the balcony window without enthusiasm. 'The day fades. To make up for the sky I will stroke my invisible herds and my own neck in turn, rest my bulk here and repeat my claims of superiority.'

'Outstanding, sir, but there is still the matter of the speech tomorrow. You can't postpone again.'

'Where's Turbot?' Rudloe kicked a floor lobster, which flew to smash against the wall. In unison the others stopped moving momentarily, then continued to scuttle. 'Bastard's probably hunkered down with his philosophy in curlers. We could use him now. A slogan with a future is a thief without parallel.'

'People are hard to quantify. Opinions differ.'

'Different people? A patchwork won't wash easy.' Rudloe frowned at the ceiling. 'We need to convince them all's for the best, in a friendly way. "Fate is fun", how about that?'

'Or convince them that wealth is actually undesirable.'

'I could smoke a cigar and start coughing really hard.

111

Say something like "These things aren't as nice as you think."'

'It would have to be done offhand,' said Gaffer pensively.

'I can do offhand. It's my middle name. "These things aren't as nice as you think." And I throw the cigar away.' Rudloe stood, stern and decided. 'Fortress your phone, Max. I prepare to be gawked at by nutters.'

A doorman entered announcing a lump-faced visitor the size of a wooden chair.

'Oh, show him in,' said the Mayor, deflating. 'It can't be any worse than that walking hammer we had in here the other week.' As he waited, he frowned at a persistent sound in his head – it was as though his sanity had come partly adrift and was bumping back and forth like a muffled clapper.

A bone coat-hanger scampered into the room, springing on to the chair opposite the Mayor's desk. Its head appeared to be made of soft clay.

'Leave us,' the Mayor told Max Gaffer, waving a weary hand. 'Whatever this is it won't put me in a savoury light.' When the door was closed, he turned to the visitor. 'Now what are you, a midget? You're not a kid, you haven't got any gills. You're not an overlevy, are you?'

'None of the above, thank you.'

'Have you covered your head with clay? How small is your head?'

'I wish please to make an offer. I will tell you the true identity of the man called Cyril. A man who though appearing simple minded yes thank you, is in fact all fouled-up with fancy hardship and split-second timing.'

'Guess I don't get this for free. State your terms.'

'Well, I want you to rename the sun.'

'The sun? Rename? To what?'

'Jonathan.'

'I beg your pardon?'

'Yes thank you, from now on people will say "lying in Jonathan" and "never look directly at Jonathan" and "Jonathan is hot today" and "where are my Jonathan glasses".'

'And instead of sunrise, Jonathan-rise.'

'You're getting the idea.'

'Idea? Now you listen to me, my lad – this sun-naming scheme of yours is bloody death for everyone. What do you think this is?'

'Thank you I . . .'

'Don't thank me, you bastard. Who the hell wants to be caught dead in Jonathan glasses? Get out of here! Max!' Gaffer instantly burst in, leaving a bit of eye-jelly in the keyhole. 'Take this amateur and dump it in the trash – it wouldn't be impolite to make fun of his arms either.'

'I will,' Gaffer grinned, advancing.

Perched atop the Tower of Nowt, Dietrich slowly scanned the town with a head like a wet clawhammer. A breeze flubbered the webbing of his wings and he shifted position, hunching so that the rills on his back pulled open.

The vista was a stained outbreak of spires and flat-tops. How was this different from the dense accretion of the creep? Only the pretence that it made sense. And didn't that up the ante? These bastards were outdoing his bandwidth. Beware the beast: Man.

Gregor hadn't returned to the Bata Motel and nobody knew where he was, so Barny, Edgy and Chloe Low went to Scardummy Garden to look at his statue for a clue. Barny was telling Chloe all about the Deadly Snake

113

Contest as they walked the gravel path between lawns striped like toothpaste. 'Misses Kennedy got two rosettes – Deadliest Viper in the Neighbourhood, of course, but she was also voted Adder Most Likely to Strike the Face. Balaclava Lewis's snake won first prize in the Relentless Horror category. Good for him. His black mamba's going through the terrible twos.'

'It's a mamba,' said Edgy, 'it'll always be terrible.'

'That's a negative attitude.'

'This snake contest of yours,' Edgy muttered close to Barny. 'You know how dodgy that is?'

'So how did you first get interested in animals, Barny?' Chloe asked.

'A dog that impressed me, which stared now and now and now, honoured me with his attention. There was no going back. That dog spoke of love.'

Edgy began whistling loudly to alert Barny to the fact that he wasn't doing himself any favours in the romance department, but Barny was oblivious. Edgy picked up some gravel from the path and pushed it into his own chin, where some of it stayed. 'A beard of bees,' he gloried. 'Yeah once you got a beard of bees you got it made in the shade Bubba.'

'It's cruel sticking bees on your chin for laughs. Why bees anyway?'

'Haven't you noticed? Half the gravel on this path is in the shape of bees.'

And so it was – the killer bees which had escaped a while ago had their own little statues here in the Garden. Barny hopped yelping on to the grass verge. 'I've been killing bees!'

'Killer bees, Bubba, killer bees!' Edgy started bounding up and down on the path. 'And I like it!'

'Leave 'em alone, you murderer, get out of it. Chloe, get up here.'

'That's amazing,' said Chloe, picking up a palmful of stone bees.

'You're treading on winged animals!'

'What about the trolls you can't help eating?' laughed Edgy.

'Those are different, they're a fungus.'

'Well I've seen them roiling their chubby limbs, my lad, and they look pretty real to me.'

'I didn't say they weren't real. I mean it, come up here.'

They walked on the grass until they entered the statue stands. Chloe was fascinated by the bee find. 'There must be a statue for every animal in Accomplice, Barny. Not just the people and those demons in the side-bushes. Even your snake and your lion. Maybe amoebas are here in the form of sand grains.'

'Amoebas are very small,' Barny conceded. 'What would happen if someone took their own statue out of the Garden?'

'That happened once but people don't like to think about it,' said Chloe. 'A man called Earfont Jackson got tired of coming out here so he took his statue home and put it in the back yard. Then he started finding it in the house when he woke in the morning. Then standing at the foot of his bed. Then one night he woke up with a pain in his arm and the statue was holding him. They were fusing together, and took almost two days to become a solid mass. We've got it at the Juice Museum.'

Edgy wasn't listening, stone bees falling one by one from his dented chin. 'Hey, Low, what do you think's best – *We Are Taunted on Two Levels* or *Taunt Us on the Double*?'

'Well, one's an observation and one's a command, I suppose. I don't know Amy very well but I'd say the command would suit her better.'

'Thank you. Hear that, Bubba? Maybe even a picture of her on the cover, with a speech balloon.'

'Here's Gregor's statue.' Barny pulled some ivy from the keglike form and brushed loose mould from the face.

'Any ideas?' frowned Edgy.

Barny peered into the hard face. 'He's smiling.'

'. . . and finally,' announced Rod Jayrod, leaning languid against a statue of a valentine corpse, 'when a man blurs, does he cease to exist?'

In a state of visible deterioration, Skitter pipped his reply: 'No.'

Instantly the Powderhouse revellers became jubilant to the rim of frothing madness, including some hooting relic who thrust his varicoloured face ahead and called above the din, 'That's me – remarkable in the world!' Impassioned crazies introduced themselves and offered advice carved into food. Skittermite shrank back as he was issued with his ash certificate and a tin crucible of useless fluff. Bespangled frauds and prancing cronies allowed no time to focus – he sought out a clear space where he could stand in wooden wonder. A boy in electric scales played in a cage which swung past terrible designs tracked in the marble wall.

Skitter peered over the writhing celebrations at Rod Jayrod, who was pouring lime from a jug. 'What now, please?' he called.

Jayrod seemed unconcerned. 'Run, scream, anything you like.' He drank, looking away.

Skittermite clutched the soapstone receptacle of fluff. He felt violated, undone. Where was his centre? Jonathan glasses? What had he been thinking?

A half-masked midget grabbed his arm and said, 'I can

tell you feel wiser. Wiser and less patient. You'll never go back.' And the little man disappeared into the crowd.

12
Petit Testament

Describe social custom with care – you may give something away

Mayor Rudloe tore drawers from his desk and flung them at the floor. 'Where's the bloody cigars?'

'You must have mislaid them,' stated Max Gaffer, smirking into his own mind. 'You'll have to improvise.'

'Improvise? Last time I improvised we all ended up dressed as otters.'

'I enjoyed that.'

'So did I, so did everyone, but my god what a predicament. Minutes to discover democracy.' The Mayor stood there staring at Gaffer in clueless silence awhile.

'The hecklers will be grateful,' Gaffer offered.

Rudloe deflated a little. 'I see. Well I've faced worse. Some brisk hectoring and all will be well.'

'Yes,' Gaffer smiled. 'Read something off a platitude form.'

Startled into hope, Rudloe knelt to thrash through the drawers again.

'Before it turns ugly.'

Rudloe looked up at the lawyer. There would be no platitude forms. He stood, straightening the varicose chains of office. Then he made a redundant gesture of dismissal, and flung through the balcony windows.

The ground below was interrupted by stooges and onlookers and other living things, some wearing leather car coats. They were sneering from the get-go, or smiling in fun like Edgy, who never missed one of these unfortunate incidents if he could help it. He had dragged Amy Gort along and Barny stood nearby with Magenta Blaze. Stancing pompously, the Mayor began with studied disdain. 'To avoid making fools of yourselves, I suggest you pretend to understand me. What do I grant you? The privilege of outrage, the freedom of fury. And in the face of my conduct, who would choose not to exercise such liberties? Thus, all is well ordered.'

The crowd parried his meaning with chunders, farts and other sonic contrivances.

'And, er, I augment nature with hallmarks. Tree birds brought to account and so on. See the stillness of the blood clock below, dry and un-nourished. You'll go to the red shed, every one of you, and give your due quotient. Flop out your wallets and pretend you've a choice. I promise you nonetheless that a destination protrudes toward your journey. I'll set up a task force and set up a task force and set up a task force. My habits are reserved for accomplishments, accomplishments, not standing here, standing talking here to you whoever you are, you people. This, though a moderate scene, I question it. That shows something, eh, that I'm radical or something? What else is there – doomed Eddie Gallo? He has never made sense and shows no signs of doing so.'

In the crowd, doomed Eddie Gallo stood seemingly immersed in the merriest thoughts.

The Mayor was getting jumpy at the fringes. A glare worried at his eyes. 'The attraction of pigeons is the legs –

they're an enigma aren't they, really? So much to do, er . . . how about this . . . let's rename the sun. Pick a name, me first, I pick Jonathan, eh? And the lucky winner will brew rain and cigarettes into deserted silhouettes of blight. Who's up for it? Eh, people? The technology already exists to consider these and other matters. Stir a blessing a thousand times, make it thick.'

'Who are you?' someone shouted up.

'You know damn straight who it is!' Rudloe barked. 'I hold this town together by the cheeks of my arse! What are you all gawking at? I stand here before you and these are the ideas I get? I'm prosperous, why aren't you? You and your meaningless antics, waving your trouble-monkeys about the place! You'll stay fooled till your body gets oaty, ears eating out to the rim-rind! Try realising then, grip out of the casket, pushing earth – if you can! Melt again upon the steps, you victims! I halve my smirk by the doorframe! Boil you all!' His face became distorted, squawking. 'You want a piece of me? The ego on you! Die, die! I'm naming this palace Rudloe Manor because I'll never leave, I'll never leave, I'll never leave!'

There was a commotion below the balcony as a brittle fiend twitched across the palace face on to the blood clock platform and began pecking out a litany of condemnation. 'Accomplice!' it screeched with a head like a corner sandwich. 'Yes please, you ! You were meant to be a domain of paradise meat thank you, but within two hours bad luck hid goldfish in my soap – I arrive to dropkick you into bedlam and you repay that trust with, yes, wandering attention or outright sleep please. Apparently evil is a subtlety beyond your grasp! The bad-luck pantomime you call society, the blood-nothing of your bodies – you and your expensive buffoonery, thank you, I . . . I feel exhausted just talking about it.'

No two expressions alike, the crowd were already shouting: 'Cyril! Cyril!'

'You are concern!' others hollered in obeisance. 'Take my trousers!'

Mayor Rudloe gripped the rail and peered down. 'Cyril? Oh pan the place why don't you. That's a lot of damp news. Democracy regulates traffic, that's all.'

The demon zigzagged with irritation. 'Damnation itself is in jeopardy! Faded labels speaking just out of reach! My mind is cracking!'

'As compared to painting a dog, charity is wearisome,' someone shouted.

'Do you think the bastard's frail enough to be withered by a photoflash of logic?' brayed the Mayor. 'I'm pretty damn sure it was this dingbat who came to me suggesting some ludicrous idea about re-naming the sun. Is that the sort of etheric funster you want to give your trousers to? Speaking sweet reason in your ear? Any organisation'll be a disgrace to Accomplice. We lead the world in chaos and bullshit.'

'Says you.'

Rudloe made a strangled sound of affront and astonishment. The rabble were getting out of hand. He switched stances in a hurried portrayal of pacific equanimity. 'Yet with due consideration my actions necessitate a rival.' He ducked afraid, an imagined rock passing his head. 'Er . . . yes, well, so I welcome Mr Cyril to the mayoral race. A few chubby children will be amused, I'm sure.'

'No!' shouted Skittermite in a sandblasted voice. 'Your arrogance has caused the air to divide up into silver beetles which attack me! Brown summer blocks into my eyes! Forests carved from mahogany!'

The Mayor nodded stoutly. 'That's right, girlfriend. You people should be ashamed of yourselves! Carving trees!' He extended the last word for a minute and a half, phasing it in and out with an open face. Skittermite meanwhile was crying out like a castaway.

'Nothing connects, nothing thank you!'

In the audience, Edgy was chuffed. 'This is the best,' he gasped with hilarity, his face bright and appreciative. 'They've both gone off their nut.'

'Hey, chump,' Amy Gort stated. 'Look what we're seeing – *we are taunted on two levels.*'

'Eh?' Edgy was suddenly worried. 'No, no, they're taunting us on the double.'

'You're wrong.'

'Does anyone need any milk later?' asked Barny.

'Tranquillity is politics reversed!' screamed Skittermite.

'Hey, they don't need to be hearing that!' stammered the Mayor, sweating like a hog. 'Cigars are b-bad, throw 'em away, no . . .'

'Fractured all,' said Skittermite with a bitter, chittering laugh. 'It's the Round One, that roiling botch of a man. Please, has there ever been an atrocity to equal him? I could have been a fine demon if it weren't for him, wingspan wiping the sky as the colour of your screams shifted into autumn. What do you say about my ribcage now? Cyril? I'm Skittermite Syrinx, Pestilent Demi-Sitch thank you! Show yourself, Round One!' And the demon began to choke with sobs. 'Won't you?' He turned and started whacking his head against the frozen clockface like a gavel.

Something gave inside the mechanism, counterweights dropping, and the big hand clicked to twelve – two doors flipped open on either side of the clockface and from each a mechanical knight was propelled on to the platform, swerving to converge on the demon.

Slumped on the back of the blue one, sated, naked and happy, was Gregor.

With each chime of the clock the knights struck down at the startled demon, twenty-four wounds wedging his flesh. A confetti of his own headblood rained past his eyes.

'Crowned for loss, what am I saying? Where am I . . . ?'

Skittermite floated from the platform into the crowd, landing flat as a cranefly.

The blood clock was in full flow, clicking smoothly.

Magenta Blaze was gaping up at Gregor. 'Now *that*,' said Barny, 'is an interesting man.'

'Well,' muttered the Mayor. 'It could have gone worse.' But as he went inside, he remembered the note in his journal, underlined three times: *No more fatal stabbings during speech!*

A crack team of bored idiots wandered away. An ambulance made of glass roared up too late.

Creeping backstage like a pantaloon executioner, Prancer Diego was pensive. He walked slow across town, looking at hot pavement, oil stains in driveways and cycads spiking from drains. Entering the shaman's yard by an overgrown side door, he blunted his nose, removed the bicycle clips from his throat, and was Beltane Carom.

13

Not Be All Right

A cliché is like a womb – we can sleep there, hide there, be safe there. And like the womb it must be abandoned if we are to reach full adulthood.

'The Aspict's back on line,' Sweeney called as Dietrich Hammerwire strode into the cavern. 'It's been an interesting few days hasn't it Dietrich? Skittermite's burnt his bridges like a good'un. You've referred to him as an upstart at every turn. And I've been menaced by a clueless mound of lard. It's the last part that worries me. We can't have just any fatso bumbling around hell cuddling the underfiends.'

'I don't think he cuddled anyone.'

'That's as may be,' said Sweeney, cheerfully dismissive. 'Those meaningless rectangles embossed on your belly – what's it all about?'

'Belly squares. What you probably don't know is these are all the rage on the street.'

'You don't care what you do, do you – not really? Are you wearing an Alice band?'

'I might be.'

'I'm in a good mood, I don't know why. Maybe it was the cake. A nice thought, that. First thing I'll do when I destroy humanity's bandwidth is eat a few of their scones and so on. There's a whole world out there – ours to empty.'

'I'm sorry, Master, but I just don't think so. It's like holding up a matchflame to the sun.'

'Oh you are one for exaggeration.'

'You haven't seen it lately. Amateurs in chains judging the horizon. Over-patient saints at the mercy of bureaucrats. Random acts of lethargy. Circumstances on the rampage.'

'Here's the Aspict,' said Sweeney as it floated down and settled, disturbing a pyramid of molars. 'Skittermite may yet surprise us.'

The Ruby cleared upon a gathering in some kind of switching yard. A muzzle-loading cannon the size of a locomotive engine had been wheeled along a rail from a funeral hanger. Streaked with backblow, swirling embellishments on the serrated barrel portrayed dismal encounter scenes. The Fusemaster Rod Jayrod stood near the cannon wearing jester-diamond vestments of black and purple. 'Who left this shiv here?' he demanded, kicking a knife away with an irritable stare at the assembly. Fuseheads stood in the wet daytime heat, many saddled with binoculars. The feinting palm trees made it a lovely scene.

'Dunk the year in dove paint, does that mean peace? I don't know.' Jayrod leant against the cannon, pensively sardonic. 'Anyway, here we are again. Cyril pecked out a few prayers with us. He was a strange fellow, thrown so far back upon his own resources he was usually off in the distance somewhere. During the catechism exam our gauges had indicated that he was a hopeless wreck. He was one of us, finally. And now, hi-jinks concluded, he's gloriously ordained for a blundering flight outside the mortal round. At birth we are meat in a rush – so should we be at death. Subtle today, forgotten tomorrow. We shall not forget our friend Cyril.'

From his vestments Jayrod produced a Velocitous

prayerbook with a black pearl cover. He regarded the pages diffidently. 'The true round is infinity.'

The assembled fuseheads answered low by rote. 'A glimpsed understanding awkward on the edge of the air.'

'Why get all bent out of shape?'

'Through our answers runs the pest of truth.'

'To the unresponsive sky volcanically delivered.'

'May he attain escape velocity.'

'With offence taken. Nostrils wild.'

'With his body we supply the sky's predation.'

'Lock and load.'

Lackeys hauled on some tarry rope – with a clank of counterbalance the cannon tipped a few degrees to the sky. The crowd recited: 'What are you going to do?'

'The only thing I *can* do,' read the Fusemaster. 'Fire our friend out of this here cannon.'

Two fusehead assistants marched toward the cannon mouth with a wooden casket. They placed this on the ground and looked down at the contents. 'A bat with a shell?' muttered one.

'Times have changed,' grunted the other. He picked up the body of Skittermite and dropped it down the cannon barrel like a broken umbrella.

'All right,' said Jayrod as they stepped back. 'Let's send this freaky-assed booger.' He removed the blue touchpaper from his lapel and pushed it into the powder vent. Then he struck a match on his arse and put it to the fuse while reading from the little book. 'Look out now, look out, look out, I'm lighting the fuse. There's gunna be one hell of a bang. Run, run.'

The cannon discharged a glaring cloud of confetti, poison gas and mental splinters from which Skittermite blurred like a dart, twisting away through the blond sky.

'Look at him go. Quick, say 'bye.'

''Bye!' called the fuseheads, waving and peering through their binoculars.

The horizon went straight for Skittermite, snapping him up like a juicy bug.

Jayrod lit a cigarette. 'That was fucking sweet.'

In the bitter cavern, Sweeney's complicated mouthparts were spread like a starflower, an insectile gape. His complexion smoked.

'I told you,' snarled Dietrich. 'I told you that skinless wonder hadn't the bite radius for a job like this. I just plain never trusted him to start with. You're too . . . *patient.*'

Sweeney locked his mouth briefly, marshalling his pride. 'Seeds following a long spine of thought, to them does it feel slow?'

'Maybe.'

'No. No, you know why we'll win? Because shadows don't have to finish. You're aware I've a cosmos of compressed monsters to redeem.'

Dietrich imagined demons swarming like leaf-cutter ants and taking a half-moon out of heaven. It felt to him like a sweet childhood dream, precocious and naive. 'You'll need them all.'

Sweeney was pensive. 'Feroce maybe, or Rammstein, what do you think?'

'The Ponce is too subtle – you need someone who'll tangle with their legs and crash them down.'

'Again with the legs. But perhaps you're right. We need an old-time bone-freezer, a shrike – Rakeman, why not? The rib ladder. There's one that doesn't need any frills such as antlers and so on. Yes, good old Rakeman – he'll turn a man's tissue to frozen vinegar.'

'I admit he's a freak of the old school, but—'

'Yes, why use a modally boned demon for a world which is, as you claim, chaos anyway?'

'It's far worse than that, Your Majesty. Throw evil at Accomplice and they spread it around like fertiliser. We're . . . *wallpaper* to them. They just fired Kermit out of a *cannon*.'

'No, there's some heads too light to use for a tetherball, that's all. Flesh is the illusion of years' duration, it'll need a while to dispel. You're a pessimist in your old age, Dietrich.'

'So regret me.'

'What did you say?'

'Nothing. I'm going to my room.'

Sweeney spoke into a face antenna. 'Pull up Demon 1,656.'

An organic booth pushed from the cavern floor in a burst of steam, a form unfolding slowly from the capsule. Rakeman, a thing of belted bones, advanced through twists of sick yellow light, its head all screams.

Dietrich slouched into his chamber, which was a migraine scramble of cobalt green. Reaching under the bed, he dragged out a travel case made from a couple of ribcages. He looked through his stuff in a desultory way, collected a couple of hammers, a faded photo of he and Sweeney mirthfully roasting a farmer, and his prize possession, the very jaw of Violaine which had said, 'There is a passion for conflict which requires no deception.' These he stowed in the case, which he hooked into place at the front of his armour. Then he opened the roof on to a vista of etheric turbulence and banged open his wings, ascending through cyanide skies.

Magenta Blaze had attached herself to Gregor but, loose and vented, he was as happy as a decal on a breast. He'd also picked up an idea from somewhere and pitched it to Stampede Products – Jonathan Glasses, the glasses which alter the visual effect of the sun. When challenged with the notion that this was an identical product to 'sunglasses', he stated with a knowing smile that much could be achieved with a change of name.

Edgy could believe it – the publishers had decided to call Amy's poetry book *Flowers Are Lovely*.

The only thing that still bothered Gregor was Barny running him down with the tricycle. 'Barny wouldn't ride a bike,' Edgy told him as they walked through town. 'He saw skybikes when he was young, the idea terrifies him, he's allergic.'

'Skybikes? Those phantom things?'

'Leg's go over to Barny's place and set things straight, eh?'

But halfway up the gangplank sat the lion. When Edgy tried to approach, the animal let out a sound like a truck igniting. They backed up, wary.

His scalp stuffed with scrawler bugs, Noam B. Turbot passed the pumps in the levy extraction shed, and entered the antique elevator. Walls of pulsing capillaries wormed upward as he sank. He strode through the silverine foyer of bleached portraits and grey decoration, and pushed through the end doors. *Disgust be a friend*, he thought as the clammy air hit him.

'Concerning hyphen five,' the Conglomerate was saying as he entered, then the multiple reaction head perked up to his presence. 'Well, it's no less an alcoholic than Noam B. Turbot.'

Turbot slipped, almost falling. The room flubbered in response.

'Yes, the floor of our game is alive. What brings you before our very select group?'

Attempting truculence, Turbot drew a shallow breath. 'For recognition. The Cyril Manifesto, yes, that masterpiece was mine. I'm entitled at least. Yes, a stab at your root-system, I've still got it in me.'

A new face awoke. 'Is that the speechwriter flapping his ashtray jaw?'

'He's claiming he wrote the Cyril tract.'

'As if we care.'

Turbot advanced into the heaving landscape of blubber and stretching astringent. 'You don't?'

'Well, duh. We know we didn't write it, that's all that matters. Life's an unhurried, casual darkness, Turbot. Learn it at last.'

Turbot was wretched. He looked about him at their trailing, fossicated organs. 'I've done stuff though.'

'Of course you have. And herein lies the reward – grief doubled, great designs of killing delusion, momentary wisdom swept away like lint in a hurricane. Now carry a little smile though choking, Turbot.'

'All right, you can say what you like about me. But I'm loyal. I've come through every time.'

'An odd victory, to be always reliable.'

'At least I was wrong about all the right things. I tried, didn't I?'

'Time to lie down, Mr Turbot.'

'In the old days—' Turbot began.

'Take me as I am,' trilled the Conglomerate, swelling, and darted a sucker at Turbot's face. 'And blame me for nothing.'

Blood shot through the throbbing cable as Turbot stood rigid, justice affronted within his dying body. Rattling, his head crumpled like a bag and puffed a cloud of dead powder. The room flushed red. Turbot fluttered, nerves firing for the last time.

The connection was broken. He tipped like a stack of old newspapers, coming apart.

*

Barny lounged in his tropical bunk, his arms about a sleeping Chloe Low. 'I love it here,' he whispered, and kissed her warm sugar skull.